FROM WINE TO WATER

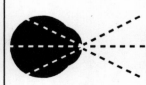

This Large Print Book carries the
Seal of Approval of N.A.V.H.

AN ANGELS AND OUTLAWS
HISTORICAL ROMANCE (#1)

FROM WINE TO WATER

CAROLYN BROWN

THORNDIKE PRESS
A part of Gale, Cengage Learning

GALE
CENGAGE Learning™

Detroit • New York • San Francisco • New Haven, Conn • Waterville, Maine • London

GALE
CENGAGE Learning™

Copyright © 2010 by Carolyn Brown.
An Angels and Outlaws Historical Romance Series #1.
Thorndike Press, a part of Gale, Cengage Learning.

LIBRARY OF CONGRESS CATALOGING-IN-PUBLICATION DATA

Brown, Carolyn, 1948–
    From wine to water / by Carolyn Brown.
        p. cm. — (Thorndike Press large print clean reads) (An
    angels and outlaws historical romance series ; 1)
    ISBN-13: 978-1-4104-3676-4 (hardcover)
    ISBN-10: 1-4104-3676-4 (hardcover)
    1. Outlaws—Fiction. 2. Sisters—Fiction. 3. Large type books.
    I. Title.
    PS3552.R685275F77 2011
    813'.54—dc22   2011011199

Published in 2011 by arrangement with Thomas Bouregy & Co., Inc.

To my cousin, Judy Chapman Jensen,
with much love!

PROLOGUE

February 1836

Like a caged Texas coyote, Tyrell Fannin paced the tiny jail cell. One end to the other took three strides, and that was the long side of the room. If he stretched his arms, he lacked only six inches to touch both walls of the narrow side. His cousin, Micah Burnet, slept on a cot on one side; his other cousin, Isaac Burnet, stared at the bars separating the cell from the room beyond it as if he could make them disappear with his stone-cold gaze.

The room beyond the bars was barely bigger than their outhouse back in Greenville, Mississippi. An oak desk took up most of the space. The chair behind it was the only other furniture in the place. Twice a day the sheriff of San Antonio came to thumb through paperwork or to push a bucket of beans and a plate of corn bread through the opening in the bars.

7

Tyrell stopped at the end of the cell and held on to the bars over the window with both hands. Dawn gave form to the bare tree limbs, presenting a black-and-white picture that looked like a child's rendering of a landscape — all lines with no softness. Spring would bring green leaves, and if they didn't get out of jail soon, it would be past planting season in Mississippi. If they lost this year's crop, they'd lose everything their parents had worked for all those years.

Tyrell heard the sheriff whistle in the early morning as he headed toward the jail. Tyrell recognized the tune and wondered how anyone could be cheerful when disaster was on the way. Mexico wasn't going to let Texas go without a fight. He'd heard on their trip to San Antonio that the merciless general Santa Anna had enlisted the help of several Indian tribes to help him wipe out resistance, and the Alamo was resistance.

The whistling stopped, but there was no jangle of keys preceding the opening of the only door into the jailhouse. Tyrell strained his ears to hear what had stopped the sheriff.

"Do you think they'll take the offer?" a stranger's voice asked.

"I think the biggest one would kill Santa Anna bare-handed if we offered to let him out of the cell. He can't stay still in there. He's going to pace the ground away, then crawl out from under."

Tyrell quickly joined Isaac on the second cot and whispered, "No matter what they offer, we're taking it. I'll fight the Mexicans and win this battle for the Texans if they'll let us out of here."

Isaac nodded seriously. "I wish we'd just stayed home."

Micah awoke on the other side of the room and stretched. When his eyes adjusted, he moaned, "I'd hoped I was dreaming. I'd do about anything in the world to get out of here."

The front door opened, and two large men quickly filled the small office. The sheriff was as round as he was tall, with a big belly hanging over his belt, a rim of gray hair around his balding pink head, and tiny, pig-like eyes that missed nothing. The other man was in uniform and stood tall, his head almost touching the low ceiling. His black hair was combed back, and worry filled his dark blue eyes. He addressed the trio in the cell.

"You two are the Burnet brothers, and you are Tyrell Fannin, their cousin. I know why you're here, and I'm here to offer you a deal. You want to go home to Greenville,

9

Mississippi, and I have a way to allow you to do that. I am Captain Robert Lavalle from Louisiana. I have three . . . three sisters I want taken to safety before this battle starts. I don't trust Santa Anna to . . ." He let the sentence trail off, as if he couldn't even utter the words.

"We'd rather stay and fight along with Texas," Tyrell said.

"Three more men won't make the difference. We'll either win by our wits and determination, or we'll lose, but these girls — women — need to be taken back to Louisiana for their own safety," Captain Lavalle said.

"But aren't most Mexicans Catholic? Santa Anna wouldn't hurt sisters, would he?" Micah asked.

Captain Lavalle opened his mouth to argue, then shut it tightly while he collected his thoughts. "I don't want to take the chance. I'm offering you your freedom. If you don't want it, you can stay in this cell another twenty-seven days for busting up the cantina and causing that brawl. It's your decision. I will provide a wagon and four horses to pull it and supplies. You want to go home to Mississippi. I want these women delivered to northern Louisiana, which is right on your way home."

"Why us? You don't know us. We're in jail. That makes us outlaws. You'd trust us to keep our word and not harm the sisters?" Isaac asked.

"I know enough," Captain Lavalle answered. "I've heard your story. A bandit shot your father in the back for the horse he was riding. You boys and your cousin here found the body, buried Mr. Burnet, and went hunting for revenge. Your chase ended here in San Antonio, but you got here a day too late. The thief had tried to rob the San Antonio bank and got himself killed in the process. In a fit of anger, you got drunk in the cantina and got entangled in a brawl with a band of Mexicans and locals. That was three days ago. You aren't such bad 'outlaws.' Besides, you managed to get here through all the obstacles in your path, so you can get back through the same. Like I said, you want to go home. I will pay you very well to get these women to their destination."

"I vote that we do this for the captain," Micah said. "I wouldn't want to see three sisters get hurt while we sit in jail."

Sit in jail. Tyrell shivered. "Isaac?" he asked.

"I'd rather be on the way home than sittin' here for a month. And we've got spring plantin' to do."

Tyrell nodded toward Captain Lavalle. "When do we leave?"

"In an hour. The wagon is loaded. The women are ready. The sheriff will give you back your horses and your gear, and your bill is paid at the livery and at the cantina. Your payment is in two saddlebags. One is for expenses along the way. The other is your money for the job. Keep the sisters safe."

"You're payin' us up front? How much?" Micah asked.

"A hundred dollars in gold," Captain Lavalle said. "And I have ways of guaranteeing that you complete your service successfully," he added meaningfully.

Micah gulped at the amount but nodded seriously. "That sounds fair. Where, exactly, are we taking them?"

"Ned Bennett's Bluff. Have you heard of it? You'll be taking them just east of there. From Bennett's Bluff they know the way and can direct you."

"That would be the plantation in the northern part of the state?" Tyrell asked.

Captain Lavalle nodded. "That's right. They'll be" — he coughed nervously, as if he was uncomfortable for some reason — "they'll be starting a small mission near there."

"Other people know they're coming?" he guessed.

"They do, and they'll be glad to see them," Captain Lavalle said. "They'll also let me know if the women *don't* arrive," he added for emphasis.

"We stopped close to that place for a night," Micah recalled aloud.

Tyrell almost smiled. Fate had been good to them. They'd be home in no time.

Captain Lavalle walked up to the bars and looked each man in the eye. "One other thing. You touch a one of those sisters in an inappropriate way, and I will make sure the coyotes and buzzards eat well when I find you."

"We're not that sort," Isaac told him. "We honor and protect women, and we sure wouldn't harm a nun, even if we aren't bent toward that faith. We attend the Protestant church over in our part of the world, but you can be sure we will be gentlemen."

"I hope your word is as good as your determination to punish the sins of the man who shot your father. Good day, gentlemen, and good luck." Captain Lavalle left, but his presence and his words lingered in the jail long after he'd shut the door behind him.

The sheriff unlocked the cell door. "Your

horses are at the stable next door. I already told Jose that the bill would be paid later today. And, boys, remember, this won't be easy. You three riding hell-bent for leather across the countryside tracking a bandit is a lot different than transporting three women through warring Indians and maybe even Santa Anna's men."

"You trying to talk us out of it?" Tyrell asked. "I thought you'd be glad to have us out of your jail and out of your town."

The sheriff nodded. "Just remember, son, sometimes things ain't what they appear. If you make a run for it with that man's money in your saddlebags and leave those women behind, I'll come after you myself. I might be old and fat, but I can still shoot straight. You be back here in an hour and ready to ride."

CHAPTER ONE

They were sitting on their horses when the wagon pulled up in front of the jail. One nun sat in the driver's seat, holding the reins and having no trouble controlling four magnificent black horses. Even in the pale light of the morning's beginnings Tyrell could see that she had a flawless, creamy complexion and a nice round face with sweet lips. With that skin and those pale blue eyes, she could have caught a man in any state in the Union.

He nodded toward her. "Good mornin', ma'am. I'm Tyrell Fannin. These are my cousins, Isaac and Micah Burnet. We will be escorting you to your destination. We'll take turns driving the wagon. Isaac is your driver today. Tomorrow Micah will drive. I will ride point on the trip. Whoever isn't driving will keep a watch behind our backs."

The nun who held the reins said, "I am Delia . . . Sister Delia. This is Sister Fairlee and Sister Tempest. We appreciate your taking us, even though it is with sadness that we leave. . . ." She stopped and swallowed hard. She hadn't wanted to leave the Alamo or San Antonio, and she sure didn't want to leave in a wagon escorted by three outlaws just bailed out of jail. But that's what their lot would be, and they'd accept it. She moved to one side of the buckboard, stepped down to the ground, and headed to the back, where Isaac was tying his horse to the rear. Isaac held out his hand and helped her up into the wagon with the other two sisters.

With a flick of the reins that cold morning in late February, they were on their way back to Louisiana. Against their wills. But they obeyed as they'd been taught, even if it did go against their grain and aggravate the sin out of all three of them.

"I hate this," Tempest whispered.

"We have to be nice. We've tempted God enough this morning, and lightning could still come out of the sky and strike us all. Just remember, there will be an end to sitting in the back of this wagon. It won't last forever. We promised Father, and we have to keep our word," Fairlee said.

Tempest shot her a look from under dark lashes. The youngest of the three, she was also the shortest with the curliest black hair, the darkest blue eyes that bordered on charcoal gray when she was angry, and the worst temper of the lot of them. She tried to control it — honestly, she did — but most of the time she failed miserably.

Fairlee grinned, which infuriated Tempest even more. Fairlee's long hair was as black as Tempest's but not nearly as curly, with just enough wave to give her misery when she pinned it into a chignon at the nape of her neck. Not that anyone could see any of their hair with the headgear that covered everything but their faces. That was the part of being a "nun" that Fairlee hated the most. Her eyes were dark blue with a black rim around the outer edge, and she was an inch or two taller than Tempest, but then, the youngest sister was only five feet two inches.

Fairlee straightened the white fabric around her face, tucking a stray black hair back at the same time. The wind was bitter that morning. Nothing between them and the cold north but a few rolling hills covered with low trees that had no leaves yet. In Louisiana the magnolias would be setting blooms, and the willows would be leafing out. Even though she didn't want to leave Texas when it was so vulnerable, she was eager to get back to Louisiana. She would have stayed willingly at the Alamo with Tempest and Delia and loaded guns or manned a post, but secretly she longed for the softer lifestyle of a more civilized world.

Delia felt every rumble of the uneven earth beneath the wagon wheels. She'd be glad when the time came that she didn't have to ride in the back like a child or, worse, like a calf being taken to market for slaughter. She should have been born a boy, and they should have let her stay in the Alamo to fight. She could shoot the eyes out of a rattlesnake at fifteen yards. Santa Anna had only to show her his beady black eyes, and his army would fall apart for lack of a leader. Even Jim Bowie and Davy Crockett, who'd arrived only two days before, had said that she'd be an asset to the shooters. But there she sat in the back of a wagon, being hauled back to Louisiana.

"Stop pouting," Fairlee whispered from behind her, one hand held close to Delia's ear.

Delia's frown and uptilted chin was the only answer Fairlee got.

Delia was not a sit-still type of woman. She liked to be in the middle of the action, getting things done. Riding along with nothing to do but wring her hands didn't sit well

18

with her. She'd at least had a book to read when they came from Louisiana to Texas two months before. That time it had been by stagecoach and had taken a month.

The stagecoach had specific destinations for each day and stopped frequently at inns for the night. But Father had said that these outlaws would most likely take them back the way the crow flew. There would be few inns if any, and often they'd probably have to sleep on the trail. The only thing Delia hated worse than sitting all day with her hands folded was making and breaking down camp.

She wished she could at least ride point with the tallest of the outlaws. He'd said his name was Tyrell Fannin. She'd heard the surname Fannin. It was fairly common, but who'd name a child Tyrell? It must be black Irish or maybe an old French name that she'd never heard before. He sat tall in the saddle with a straight back, holding his head high. He was a lean man with a more angular face than those of his two cousins, who appeared to be younger than the twenty-five she guessed him to be.

The younger one, Micah, rode behind the wagon and kept a watchful eye on their trail. His hair was medium brown and needed cutting. His eyes reminded Delia of pecan shells. Light brown with little dark flecks. It appeared that he knew the business of being the lookout and took his job seriously.

Isaac was definitely Micah's brother. They looked alike, but Isaac was much more serious. The sunlight picked up red highlights in his dark brown hair. When he'd helped her up into the wagon, Delia noticed that his eyes were a dark, mossy green. He was slightly heavier than Micah, with upper arm muscles that strained the seams of his coat. He didn't offer comment on the countryside but kept the horses moving along at a steady speed. They'd used the stagecoach trail leaving San Antonio, but, just as Father said, they soon left it and began to travel "as the crow flies." Straight out across the countryside, headed northeast.

"This isn't the way we came out here," Tempest observed.

"Tyrell is a tracker, and he knows how to get around Santa Anna's forces. He'll keep you safe," Isaac said.

Before Delia could comment, dozens of men on horseback burst from a wood and surrounded the wagon, guns drawn.

"Well, those were words in vain. How are Tyrell and Micah going to protect us now?" she demanded. "They're both cut off from us."

The leader of the men, a short Mexican with a rifle pointed straight at Isaac, lowered it carefully when Delia stood up. He motioned to another man and barked several sentences, then pointed at Isaac.

"My captain wants to know what you are doing in this place with three nuns," the second soldier said.

"Transporting them to Louisiana," Isaac said.

"From San Antonio? From the mission there?"

Isaac nodded.

"Who sent them?"

"Father sent us. He was afraid for our lives with the battle that is coming," Delia interjected.

The Mexican soldier turned and translated what had been said, gesturing at Isaac and then at Delia.

The leader didn't look very happy, but he lowered his gun a little farther and narrowed his eyes. He spoke rapidly, and the translator nodded.

"He says to tell you that Santa Anna would never hurt a nun but that it is wise for you to go to a farther mission at this time. We will send a scout ahead of you to spread the word that you are to have safe passage through our armies. We would never harm an angel of God. But the Indians might have different views. We will take you to safety. They respect us," he said.

"Bless you for your offer, but we will travel on with these men." Delia crossed herself and sat back down. Her knees were shaking. There were more men here than there were soldiers in the Alamo. They'd heard that hundreds were joining Santa Anna, but until that moment it was only rumor. Now she had no doubt that the tyrant's troops were crawling over Texas like ants on watermelon juice. If the Alamo had a stone still standing when the smoke settled, it would be a miracle.

Abruptly the men disappeared into the trees like fog on a sunny morning.

Fairlee let out a gasp. "Thank goodness they were Catholic."

Tempest giggled. "Thank goodness we were Catholic."

Isaac had never heard a nun giggle. Of course, he'd never really talked to a nun. He had seen a few in their black-and-white attire from a distance, and they'd always been very stern looking. He didn't think the ones he'd seen would laugh over something as serious as what had just happened.

Tyrell had ridden back to the wagon.

Micah, too, caught up. "I thought we were

goners. I didn't see a thing coming until they were all around the wagon. I figured they'd shoot us all."

Tyrell nodded. "What were they talking about?" he asked Isaac.

"Santa Anna's men wanted to know what we were doing with the nuns. I told him, and he said he'd send a scout ahead to let the others know to leave us alone," Isaac explained.

They'd barely gone a mile before more Mexican soldiers approached. This time a translator rode forward with a man who radiated power. All the soldiers around him seemed to shrink in his presence, regarding him with a reverence befitting God. Confidence rode on his shoulders as comfortably as did the smile on his face.

He spoke, and the translator said, "El Presidente Santa Anna wanted you to know personally that he would never harm a nun. He wants you to bless his mission and pray for his success."

Delia hated to even pretend such a thing, but their lives depended on her at that moment. She grasped the rosary hanging from her waist and bowed her head, fingering the beads as she moved her mouth as if in silent prayer.

Santa Anna did not open his eyes or look

up for several moments after she finished. The soldiers around him kept guns trained on the Burnets and Fannin while Santa Anna received his blessing.

Finally Santa Anna nodded and spoke. The man with him said, "El Presidente doesn't understand why you are being transported so rudely. He is willing to shoot these men and give you a proper carriage to carry you to your destination."

"Jesus went into the city of Jerusalem on a donkey's back," Delia improvised. "Are we better than our Lord? The Virgin Mary slept and gave birth in a stable. We would not presume to be better than the mother of Christ or our Savior. This wagon and escort is fine," she said.

When Santa Anna heard the words, he nodded.

"We wish you safe passage to your new mission, and we thank you for the prayer," the man said.

Less than half a day out of San Antonio, Delia had already shaken in her shoes more than if she'd stayed behind and hefted a rifle to her own shoulder to defend the Alamo. Surely God would give them a peaceful journey the rest of the day.

"That was Santa Anna?" Tempest asked when the wagon started rolling again.

"I guess so," Delia said.

"I expected someone much bigger and older. He's not much older than we are, is he? And he's actually kind of pretty," Fairlee said.

"He wouldn't be pretty if he had a gun in Father's face, would he?" Tempest protested.

"Even Santa Anna wouldn't kill a priest," Isaac said from the buckboard.

"But Father is —" Tempest began.

Delia touched her arm and shook her head.

"I . . . I should hope he wouldn't," Tempest said weakly.

"How much longer is it until we stop to stretch our legs?" Fairlee asked before Tempest could say anything else.

"Not long," Tyrell answered.

Twice in one morning he'd thought they'd be shot down like dogs in the street. He wanted out of this area before they stopped for anything. He rode on ahead, his heart still pounding in his chest. The men at the old mission in San Antonio didn't stand a chance against so many Mexicans. Already they'd seen more than three times the number of soldiers in the Alamo. How many more were hiding behind every tree?

Tyrell was glad he'd agreed to take the

job. Oddly enough, the nuns were providing him and his cousins safe passage through the enemy lines. However, he reminded himself as he rode ahead, if they didn't have the sisters traveling with them, they wouldn't stand out like a fox in a henhouse and probably would have been able to maneuver through the lines without being stopped.

In a small clearing in the middle of a pecan grove close to a creek, he called a halt by raising his hand. Isaac pulled up on the reins. Micah rode up from the rear. The nuns wasted no time getting out of the wagon and heading away from the campsite.

"Where are you going?" Tyrell called out.

Delia turned around and glared at him.

He blushed crimson. "Don't stray too far. We'll start a fire and set up for a small meal. You do have provisions, don't you?"

"We do, and we'll get them out when we return." She raised her voice so that she could be heard as she stalked away.

"That was embarrassing," Tempest said.

"And I'm sure we'll have more awkward moments like that between here and home," Delia said.

Tempest nodded. "What on earth did you pray for when that man wanted a blessing?"

"That he would die an easy death and not

suffer and that all his men would lose courage and run from the battle," Delia said.

"That wasn't a blessing," Fairlee argued.

"It was the best I could do on a moment's notice. At least I didn't ask that he be shot in the leg with a round that caused gangrene and die a screaming death while a doctor cut off his leg at the hip. Or I didn't ask God to let a Texan shoot him in the belly and for the wound to fester and maggots to settle into it," Delia said.

"I suppose you did give him a blessing, then," Tempest said. "Would you two please hurry? I've got my legs crossed."

"Is that any way for a nun to talk?" Delia asked as she pulled up her clothing under the habit and adjusted the rosary beads hanging from her belt.

"No, it's not, and I *am* glad to be a nun this day. If we weren't, we probably would have been hauled off for those men to treat shamefully," Tempest said.

"They wouldn't treat me any way but like a lady — or else," Fairlee said.

"Or else what? What could one little woman like you do?" Delia asked.

"Die, probably, but I wouldn't go to face God by myself. There'd be a few Mexicans coming up behind me, and I'd laugh when God sent them all straight to hell."

"That's not a sweet nun's spirit. You'll have to pray for forgiveness. You might have to say a prayer for each bead and then another one as you count backward," Delia told her.

"You say them for me. I'm not in much of a mood to be praying," Fairlee said.

"Y'all better be praying and giving thanks that we got out of those two scrapes as well as we did. I'm hungry, and I'm not looking forward to days and days of this riding in a wagon stuff. Why can't nuns just ride horses like real women instead of in a stupid wagon?" Tempest asked.

"If we ever get back to Louisiana, I'm not leaving again," Fairlee said.

"Nor I," Delia agreed.

They looked at Tempest, who said, "Heck, this is the most fun I've had in my whole life. I hate riding in a wagon when I could be on a horse, leaving everyone in my dust, but you've got to admit, it's already been exciting. Just think. We can tell people that we actually saw Santa Anna, and you blessed him!"

Delia looped her arm through Tempest's and said with mock seriousness, "Fun and excitement are not a part of a nun's life, Tempest. You need to pray hard to overcome these tendencies toward adventure."

Tempest burst out laughing as they emerged from the thicket, arm in arm. The girls' eyes, various shades of blue, were twinkling, and their faces were alight with merriment.

When Tyrell saw them, he jerked off his worn felt hat and slapped his leg with it. Nothing could be funny, not after the morning he'd endured. They'd all narrowly avoided death, and they were laughing?

"Oh, did you think we were crying out for help? Tempie does have a shrill laugh, but we're fine," Fairlee said when she saw the concern on the men's faces.

Tyrell scowled. "What's so funny?"

"We're just glad to be alive. It's a normal reaction when you've had the wits frightened out of you twice in one morning," Delia explained.

"Is it a sin to laugh?" Tempest asked.

"No, but you are women of God. You're supposed to be serious, aren't you?" Micah said.

Fairlee changed the subject. "You're all grumpy because you're hungry. Did you have any breakfast this morning?"

"No. Captain Lavalle came to the jail, and we had to get ready to leave with you in a hurry," Micah said.

Delia marched past the men and straight

to the wagon. She brought out a basket filled with biscuits stuffed with ham and scrambled eggs along with a pot. "While we eat, it might be nice if you'd put some water into this pot and set it on the fire to boil so we can have a cup of coffee. It will chase away the chill and keep us all alert this afternoon."

Micah took the pot from her and headed toward the creek to fill it. Minutes later, with a biscuit in one hand and a coffeepot in the other, he had a new, if somewhat grudging, respect for the women in the black-and-white habits.

Tyrell took another look at the wagon. "You got any canteens? If so, you might want to fill them. I have no idea how far it'll be until we find water again."

Delia handed him three new canteens. He followed Micah toward the creek. She stared after him. He was well mannered and responsible. It was hard to think of him as an outlaw. Well, if the story about him and his cousins chasing down the man who'd killed their father and uncle was true, perhaps he wasn't such a cold-blooded outlaw after all.

When she had heard they were being entrusted into their care, she'd shuddered at the idea of outlaws taking them all those miles back to Louisiana, through Indians fighting with the Mexicans as well as against one another — tribes and tribes of them with different ideas about life. At least they hadn't completely banded together against the white man. Had they done that, they might still be in control of the vast lands making up the United States of America.

"We are nuns, and he's a man. Don't you look at his backside like that," Tempest whispered.

"I'm not looking at him like that," Delia declared vehemently.

"Yes, you were. Denying it is lying, and God might strike a nun deader'n a rock for that. Admit it, Delia. You were looking at Tyrell's backside as he walked away," Tempest teased.

Delia blushed, and there was no way to hide it. Her hair was stuffed up under her headgear, and her face glowed so red that she felt it was on fire. "Stop talking about things like that. Women, much less nuns, do not discuss men's backsides."

"God made backsides, didn't he?" Tempest said. "Why else would He make them so exciting, if women weren't supposed to look at them?"

"Shh!" Fairlee hushed her when she saw Micah and Tyrell returning.

Delia hiked up her black skirt enough to get back into the wagon. Micah and Tyrell averted their eyes so they wouldn't see her ankles. She set about removing a plate with a cake on it and pulling things from the basket — more biscuits and thick slices of ham and cheese. "This should do for the noon meal and keep us until we stop for the night. We'll boil beans at that time to use for tomorrow's noon and supper. We brought a heavy pot for that purpose."

"Then we should eat fairly well," Tyrell said.

Isaac and Micah grinned.

Tempest laughed at the men's obvious delight.

Delia shot her a look that was meant to shut her up but only made her laugh harder. "Help me get this food ready."

Isaac decided he could have liked those two younger nuns if they'd just been plain old girls instead of nuns.

Micah figured they were all slaphappy from relief at surviving two scares that morning.

Tyrell didn't care if they laughed or cried as long as they had food. After three days of nothing but beans and corn bread in the jail cell, that cake looked so good, he could have cried.

Manners kept Delia from telling the men that if they ate that heartily every day, they'd run out of supplies in less than a week. They'd simply have to hunt down their suppers in the future. She kept her silence, and they polished off half the cake and food that should have lasted two days, not one meal. When they stopped for the night, she'd have to make a double batch of biscuits to keep them going the next day.

"Is that all food under the canvas covers in the wagon?" Micah asked.

Delia answered with one word. "No."

"What's in there, then?"

"Supplies of a different sort. Are you Catholic?" she asked bluntly.

"No, I'm Protestant."

"Then you wouldn't understand what's under there," she retorted.

Tyrell didn't care what the canvas hid. He just hoped they could protect it all the way to Louisiana. "Better walk around the wagon a few times to stretch your legs. It's going to be a long afternoon. We won't stop again until dark."

The afternoon was uneventful. Tyrell kept to the northeast. Twice he flushed a rabbit and reached for his gun but then thought better of it. The noise could bring down more of Santa Anna's men, and they had plenty of food for supper. Just before dark he saw a white-tailed buck standing close enough to shoot, but again he decided against it. Tomorrow evening they'd be close to forty miles away from San Antonio if they kept up the pace he'd set for them. That would be soon enough to start hunting for their daily meat.

They made camp in a clearing with no water. The women brought out the food again, and everyone ate their fill. The nuns excused themselves and went back to the wagon, where they untied bedrolls and shoved them underneath the wagon without so much as a good night to any of the men.

Tyrell took first watch and was surprised to see Sister Delia remove her headgear before she settled into her bedding. Her hair was as black as the night and pinned securely into a bun at the nape of her neck. Without the stiff white fabric all around her face, she looked even younger and more beautiful. He'd figured they'd have some kind of prayer vigil or do something holy before they retired, but they'd simply whispered to one another for a while and then fell asleep.

For the next two hours he gave himself a severe lecture. Sister Delia had given her life to God's service, and even though he didn't believe in that, he had no right to impure thoughts concerning her perfect bow of a mouth. He checked the time on the pocket watch his father had left him when he died. It was time to awaken Micah, but Tyrell wasn't sleepy, so he let his cousin doze another hour before making him roll out.

By the time Tyrell was yawning, he nudged Micah, who came awake instantly, asking, "Anything happenin'?"

"It's quiet. Here's the watch. Give it an hour, and get Isaac up. I couldn't sleep, so you had an extra hour."

Micah picked up his rifle and leaned against the same tree that Tyrell had chosen for a watch spot. Transporting nuns to safety was the strangest job he'd ever taken on. Chasing the bandit who had killed his father for a horse had kept his heart racing. The fight in the cantina had spiked his energy. But that morning he'd learned real fear when he thought those Mexicans were going to kill them all.

He was twenty-two years old. His friends back in Mississippi were mostly married — some already had two or three kids — but no woman had held Micah's attention long enough for a proposal. It was the same with Isaac. At twenty-three, he'd said he'd die a

35

bachelor if a woman didn't set his heart to racing more than seeing a crop of cotton coming up out of the ground did.

Tyrell was a different story. He was twenty-eight and still unmarried, but there was a woman in his past. Back when he was twenty, Lucy Adams had stolen his heart — then broken it badly. Lucy was seventeen that summer Tyrell proposed to her. She said she'd marry him, but then she eloped with Walter Sweets, a fellow from New York who worked for the government. He took her north, and that's where they still lived. She hadn't come back to Mississippi to see her momma even one time, but then, that's the way things were. A woman couldn't go that far away and expect to come home on a whim.

It was probably for the best. Whenever Micah remembered the way Tyrell had looked eight years before, when Lucy ran away, he wanted to choke the woman until her eyes popped out. And Walter, well, he'd better just stay on up there with his big-shot government job and friends, because if he ever came back to Mississippi, Micah intended to give him the whipping he deserved. Loving Lucy, even eloping with her, wasn't a sin, but he should have been big enough to talk to Tyrell and set things straight before they left.

He glanced at the nuns asleep under the wagon. Too bad he couldn't wake up that sassy one named Tempest and make *her* stand watch for a couple of hours. He really, really didn't like her. She was entirely too flighty for a woman of God — giggling all the time and looking him right in the eye. Even women of the night didn't act that way with a man. Nuns were supposed to be dignified and godly. Sister Tempest had a long way to go before she fit that bill.

He gave Isaac an extra hour, woke him in the early hours of the morning, handed him the watch, and went back to sleep instantly.

Isaac checked the women, surprised to see that Sister Delia had removed part of her habit and was sleeping with her hands under her chin. She didn't look nearly as formidable without the white band around her face. She was actually kind of pretty, with that black hair, but he'd already made up his mind not to like any of them.

Sister Delia suddenly looked up at him as if she could see all the way to the bottom of his soul. He could imagine her telling the whole world about the first kiss he'd gotten out behind the barn. It had been with Nellie Barnstall, and he'd been fifteen. He'd thought maybe he should ask her to marry him, since he'd kissed her, but she married the preacher's son before he could get up the courage to ask her. Then there was that time he took a piece of licorice from the jar at the general store and didn't pay for it. Sister Delia looked as if she knew all about that too.

No, sir, Isaac Burnet didn't like those nuns. He just wanted to take them to their new mission and be rid of the lot of them. Then he was going home to Greenville to the place he and his brother and cousin held in common, now that their fathers were dead.

CHAPTER TWO

Tyrell watched the sun rise over the treetops in Cedar Creek. The place was barely more than a village, but according to the innkeeper, six years before a man by the name of Addison Litton and his wife had been granted a league of black dirt on either side of the creek. The innkeeper and his wife had bought enough property from the Littons to build the inn the year before, and the small community was trying to entice a preacher to come to their area. They'd already started a school and hired a teacher for the fall session. Hopefully, after Texas whupped all the Mexicans, they'd have a peaceful little community that more and more people would flock to.

Tyrell figured they'd made good time that week and had settled into a routine that was working for the bunch of them, nuns and men alike. Up in the morning before dawn, breakfast over and gear packed as the sun came up, on the road until the midday mealtime, when they stopped for no more than an hour to let the horses graze, rest, and have a drink. Then more driving until nightfall. They'd made at least fifteen miles every day. If they kept up that pace, they'd be in Louisiana a full week earlier than he'd expected.

After that first day, when they'd been surrounded by Santa Anna's men twice, things had gone smoothly. They'd encountered Indians a couple of times, but they'd been friendly enough and had allowed them to move on with no problems. Maybe they respected holy people, no matter what or whom.

He'd always been an early riser, whether he slept on the ground with his saddle for a pillow or in a bed. The nuns had seemed almost giddy at the sight of an inn and had immediately ordered a bath brought up. That was the last he'd seen of them, but the walls were thin, and he'd heard them stirring around in their room before he came down for breakfast.

The proprietor of the inn's wife, who was also cook and cleaning lady all rolled into one, set a plate of ham and eggs before him. He slathered a biscuit with butter and bit off a chunk. It wasn't as good as Sister

Delia's bread, but it wasn't bad. He hadn't had eggs since that first day on the trip, so they tasted really good. He'd just polished off everything on the plate when he heard footsteps on the narrow wooden staircase. Seeing three sets of trouser-clad legs descending, he looked out the window again. The nuns would be down in a little while. Sister Delia always arose at about the same time Tyrell did.

The window was dirty, but then, the man and woman who ran the place were busy keeping guests happy with their beds, baths, and food. They probably didn't even see the grime stuck to the windowpanes and were just grateful to have real glass in the frames. Tyrell had pushed the nuns to keep riding until they reached Cedar Creek. One of the Indians they'd met along the trail spoke enough English to tell him that up to the north was a white man's sleeping place and village.

A movement near his elbow caused him to look around. The three men had stopped at his table and were standing there, waiting. They must have arrived at the inn very late, because it had been nearly dark when Tyrell and his group had reached the place. And he must've been really tired, because he hadn't heard any newcomers' boots on

41

the stairs, and he was a light sleeper.

One of the men said, "We need to talk."

The voice was high and feminine, and Tyrell figured him for a youngster. He blinked three times before his brain registered what his eyes were seeing. All the muscles in his jaw went slack, and he had to force his chin not to land on his chest.

"What the hell?" he gasped.

They all three pulled out chairs and sat down at his table.

"W-What are you doing?" he stammered.

"I said, we have to talk. To begin with, we are not nuns. We're not even Catholic," Sister Delia said.

She wore trousers that fit her as if they'd been made especially for her, but that wasn't possible. Women wore dresses, and when they did have a need to put on pants, it wasn't out in public, and they were not tailored to them. Her hair was pulled up on top of her head and twisted into a knot. Her shirt was coarse broadcloth in a nondescript blue and buttoned up the front, the buttons on the wrong side to be a woman's blouse. Well-worn riding boots reached her knees.

"You lied to me?" Tyrell said through clenched teeth.

Tempest, who was dressed identically to her sisters, shook her head. "We never told a single lie. We just let you believe what you wanted. When Father went to the jail to talk to you outlaws about taking us home, he said we were sisters. We are. You thought he meant Catholic nuns. It was an ingenious idea, actually, and he'd made us dress that way to keep us all from being killed. And it worked. So get off your high horse about a lie."

The innkeeper's wife set three plates before the used-to-be nuns. She didn't cotton to women looking like the three of them did, especially when they had come decked out as nuns. God should strike them all dead for pretending to be nuns — but not until they were well on their way to wherever they were headed. She didn't want three dead bodies in her dining room. Besides, she'd made a good deal with them for their wagon and a new big pot for the kitchen.

"What's this all about?" Tyrell demanded.

"Captain Lavalle is our father. Our mother died six months ago, and even though Texas is a wild place, we decided to come live with him. But Father says that the battle with Santa Anna is going to be a bad one," Delia said, "and he wanted us to be safe."

The innkeeper eavesdropped from the other side of the room. Information was often as important a commodity as food, and the story of nuns coming into his inn and leaving as wild women wearing trousers would make a funny tale.

He drew near to the table and said, "That one down in San Antonio? Mexicans got that place under siege. Have had all week. Santa Anna shut it off a week ago today. Ain't nothing comin' out of there, at least not alive. And ain't nothin' goin' in neither. He's goin' to starve 'em out."

"Guess Father was right," Tempest said worriedly. "But I'm certain that he and his men will come through all right."

"You all come from thataway?"

"We did," Fairlee said.

"Dressed as nuns. That was a mighty smart thing. Old Santa Anna wouldn't harm a nun," he said.

"That's what Father said, and he was right. We met Santa Anna our first morning out," Fairlee told him.

The innkeeper started. "Was he a huge man with a black mustache and beard? Did he look like the devil?"

"He was a nice-looking young man, but I hope Father shoots him dead," Delia said. Then she turned her attention back to Tyrell. "After we have breakfast, we will meet you on the front porch. You were paid to take three sisters to Louisiana. And that we are."

Tyrell could have eaten nails at that point. Rudely, without a word of excuse, he pushed his chair back and went outside.

A chilly wind had kicked up from the north. He lit a cigar and watched the smoke swirl around as it dissipated. The cigar gave him something to do with his hands; the tobacco calmed his frayed nerves.

Isaac and Micah joined him in a few moments, both of them as shocked as he'd been a few minutes earlier.

"You see the nuns? They're dressed like menfolk — and right out in public like that! They're . . ." Micah said.

"I saw them. They're not nuns. They were just dressed like that to get out of San Antonio safely. Captain Lavalle is actually their father," Tyrell said.

"I'll be danged," Isaac said. "I knew there was something different about them women. All the nuns I ever seen looked like they'd been suckin' on lemons. What're we goin' to do now?"

"We signed on to take three 'sisters' to Louisiana. Don't reckon it matters if they're of the cloth or dressed like men. Burnets and Fannins are only as good as their word. We've been paid. We'll deliver the goods.

But we don't have to like it — or them — for not telling us the truth. We could have played along with them, if that's the way they wanted it. They didn't have to lie to us," Tyrell said.

"That youngest one, Sister Tempest, is going to be a handful," Micah said.

Tyrell shot him a look. "They're all going to be a fistful of trouble. You want the responsibility for 'Sister' Tempest?"

"Why would you do that to me? Did I do something wrong?" Micah asked.

"He's just mad 'cause he got took," Isaac said. "We'll *all* take *all* of them to Louisiana. Ain't none of us goin' to pair off and take on one apiece. Ain't no way I want that kind of thing. I wasn't too fond of 'em when they were nuns, and I sure don't like 'em much now. Women dressin' like that ain't decent. I'm going inside and havin' some breakfast. We still ridin' out at daybreak like always?"

Tyrell nodded and puffed on the cigar.

Isaac opened the door, and the three women marched out. His stomach growled with hunger, but he wouldn't have missed the ensuing argument for anything. He closed the door and leaned on the jamb.

"Okay, here's what happened. We promised our father, Captain Lavalle, that we would stay in our habits for a week — long enough to get by Santa Anna's riders. Yesterday was a week. The horses that pulled the wagon were chosen for us to ride, with one to carry supplies. Didn't you wonder what was going on when you saw those good horses pulling a wagon that a mule could have pulled? We've made a deal with the innkeeper. Sold him the wagon and the big black cooking pot. Our horses will be saddled and ready by the time you finish your morning meal," Delia said.

Tyrell drew in another lungful of tobacco smoke and glared at the women. All of them had jet black hair and shades of blue eyes. Delia's were the lightest and her hair the straightest. Fairlee's hair was slightly wavy, and her eyes were the color of the summer sky. Tempest's hair was kinky curly, springing out of the bun on top of her head and framing her face. Her eyes were a dark blue that was almost gray at times. Tyrell already knew all about their eyes and their faces. It was the rest of them that surprised him.

"We're dressed like this because we don't ride sidesaddle. Father taught us to ride and shoot like boys when we were young. We'll take care of our own horses and supplies. We could probably take ourselves to Louisiana, too, but it wouldn't be proper," Delia said.

Tyrell chuckled.

Delia narrowed her eyes and took three steps forward until she was toe to toe with him. "Don't laugh at us. We could take ourselves home and get there quicker than with you outlaws, but Father thought we needed an escort."

His face was set in stone when he looked down at Delia. "We've been paid to take you home, and we'll keep our word. Don't expect us to like it or to pamper you. Now that you've gotten rid of the wagon and plan to ride with us, just get ready to keep up."

Delia narrowed her eyes. "Mr. Fannin, there's not a man alive who could outride or outshoot a Lavalle woman. We'll try not to hurt your pride too much, but don't expect us to slow down for you. We are eager to be home."

Micah almost swallowed his tongue. He'd never heard a woman stand up to Tyrell like that. Either she was crazy or just plumb dumb. Either way, he didn't look forward to the days ahead. What should have been a fairly easy trip across Texas now promised to be a battle bigger than the one down south. After a challenge like that, Tyrell would have no recourse but to show the woman, Delia, that she'd been a fool to say such a thing.

"We will ride out at dawn like always. Today we will make twenty-five miles before we stop for camp," Tyrell said slowly.

"Only twenty-five? I was thinking if those clouds don't start dumping rain on us, we might go a little farther. No sense in lolly-gagging around, looking at the trees. We have trees in Louisiana and can sit under them at our leisure," Delia said.

Fairlee bit back a groan. She'd be saddle-sore and miserable if Tyrell pushed them twenty-five miles. He'd been a tower of anger since he realized he'd been duped. Delia wasn't one to back down, but then, neither was Fairlee. Still, she hated the idea of the day ahead.

Tyrell snuffed out his cigar on the porch before shoving the rest of it into his shirt pocket. "Your job is to keep up and not whine. Mine is to escort you home. Looks like clouds are rolling in from the southwest. If you haven't got a slicker in your saddle-bags, you're about to be wet and miserable."

"Don't be worrying about the Lavalle girls. We know how to prepare for anything. Ya'll go on and have some breakfast. We'll be sitting on our horses, ready to ride when you are," Delia said.

"I'll believe it when I see it." Tyrell stalked around her and back into the dining room.

Isaac and Micah followed him.

Delia opened her mouth to smart off at Tyrell Fannin but decided against it. She'd let him have the last word that morning, but it would not happen again.

"Okay, girls, let's go unload the wagon and saddle up. We've got a point to prove, and we will do it without a whimper. Today will probably be the worst. Fannin will push us and be an old bear. But tomorrow will be better," Delia said. "He'll get used to us."

"It'll take an hour to load our things," Fairlee said.

"We've got about twenty minutes, so work fast," Delia said.

Tempest moaned. "It was easier bein' a nun."

"Run upstairs and get those habits. I want them shoved down into a saddlebag. Who knows when we might need them again?" Delia told her.

"We wore them a whole week. If we need them again, then Micah and Isaac can pose as nuns. I'm finished with those flapping things," Fairlee said.

What started as one of Tempest's giggles grew to three women laughing so hard that the noise rang through up and down the street of Cedar Creek. Tempest was still giggling a few minutes later when she ran past the men having breakfast and up the stairs to retrieve the habits.

"Running like a schoolboy," Isaac grumbled. "She's old enough to be married and have kids, and that's not the way a lady acts."

"That's *why* she's not married," Micah said. "None of 'em will ever catch a husband unless they straighten up."

Tempest waved as she ran back down the stairs and out the front door, black habits in her arms.

"Guess they've found a use for the nuns' things," Tyrell said.

"If they put them back on, I'm for leaving them behind. Now that I know they aren't nuns, I don't want to be around when they masquerade. I ain't that fast when it comes to dodgin' them lightning bolts God's sure to shoot down on them," Micah said.

"Me, neither. I'll take the rear guard every day if they put on them habits again. That way, when God strikes them dead, He won't hit me too," Isaac said seriously.

In the livery stable the three women worked efficiently and rapidly. Delia jerked the canvas covers off three saddles and enough gear to fill the saddlebags. In unison each woman picked up a saddle and headed toward a stall. Minutes later they each led a black horse out, ready for the day's ride. Then they carefully loaded their saddlebags with personal items and ammunition. That finished, they began to load the supply horse with what they'd need to make camp — flour, sugar, coffee, and more ammunition. With luck they could restock every few days along the way. Meat along the trail should be plentiful. Delia had seen several deer and rabbits, along with squirrel and quail. They wouldn't go hungry. She shoved her rifle into the scabbard on the saddle, crammed a new black felt hat onto her head, and mounted up.

Fairlee was only a minute behind her. Tempest was the slow one. She took one more minute. Because of that, she'd be responsible for the packhorse that day. She tied his reins to the back of her saddle and sighed. She had to learn to stop looking at her sisters to see if they were ahead of her and focus on the job at hand. Tomorrow, by golly, Fairlee was taking care of that pack-horse, even if Tempest had to get up an hour early.

Without a word they rode out together and were waiting in front of the inn when the men came out the front door and headed toward the livery stable.

Tyrell glared at Delia.

She returned the look.

It was better than getting the last word by far.

CHAPTER THREE

Tyrell took the lead as usual, and the rest of the riders fell in behind him — Delia, Fairlee, Isaac, Tempest with the supply horse behind her, and Micah bringing up the rear. They rode hard without talking until they crossed the Colorado River and reached the town of Bastrop. It was almost noon, so Tyrell allowed thirty minutes for them to have a hot meal at a local inn.

The proprietor gave them a bit of town history as they ate. Delia listened with one ear and wolfed down her food. She was already weary to the bone, and the day was only half done. After five minutes of talking, the innkeeper wanted to know what they could tell him about San Antonio.

Delia kept her silence and let Tyrell talk as much as he wanted. Though he left out the part about the nuns and actually meeting Santa Anna, he explained that he was escorting the three Lavalle sisters back to their plantation in Louisiana because San Antonio was unsafe.

"You were lucky women to get out of there and smart to dress like men. Keep your faces down and let your hats cover them, and you'll stay out of trouble," the innkeeper advised.

A scathing remark about not needing protection was on the tip of Delia's tongue, but she held it back. They finished their meal within the allotted half hour and were back in the saddle when the sun reached its highest point. Tyrell took the lead at a steady clip, and they rode along a trail that was little more than two ruts for stagecoach wheels for thirteen miles to a crossroads.

Tyrell drew up short, and everyone else did the same. He crooked a leg over his saddle horn and studied the sun. It wasn't nearly dusk, but he was dog tired. They'd ridden more than twenty miles, but his pride kept him from calling it a day. He'd teach those Lavalle sisters to test his mettle.

"Which way are we going?" Delia asked.

"We can go east for a while and follow the stage ruts or follow that smaller and less used path and keep going northeast," he said.

"Which way will get us there faster?" she asked.

He pointed toward the northeast.

"Then that's the way we should go," she said.

"It's rough. Remember, you asked for it," he said.

Delia thought she'd fall out of the saddle by the time dusk set in and he stopped in the middle of a stand of scrub oak trees. She wanted to rub the numbness out of her backside when she slid off the horse but figured that gesture would surely set off mocking by Tyrell and his kin. She saw to the horse's needs before her own, removing the saddle and bridle, tethering him to a stake so he could graze, and rubbing him down with dry grass. She watered him from her canteen.

"What's for supper?" Micah asked.

"Whatever you can scrounge up," Tempest said curtly.

"We brought biscuits and ham from the inn this morning. Since we had a cooked meal at noon, we can eat that for supper," Delia said.

"You mean we've got to share with them?" Tempest asked.

"They don't know the rules. We'll share today," Delia chided.

Tyrell raised an eyebrow. "Rules?"

Delia intoned her father's steadfast travel

56

instructions. "Rules of the road. Number one: Don't assume anyone else is going to take care of you. Just because we are women doesn't mean we have to cook and clean for you. Just because you are men doesn't mean you have to take care of our horses and gear. Number two: Take care of yourself at all times. Don't expect someone else to be your savior. What if he gets killed? Number three: Obey the first two rules."

Tyrell almost wished they were back to traveling fifteen miles each day and the ladies were still nuns. He'd sure miss the cooking.

"You mean your father taught you to ride and survive in the wild?" Micah asked. In his world women cooked. They cleaned. They were cherished and loved. They did not wear men's trousers, and they rode sidesaddle. And they most surely did not learn survival in the woods.

"And the learning was good for us," Delia said.

She took biscuits stuffed with ham from her saddlebags and passed out two for each person. When they'd eaten, she passed around sugar cookies. That's all she had, and it would have to do until the next day, whether the men were still hungry or not.

"Where will you all be sleeping? There's

no wagon to protect you anymore," Tyrell asked.

"Same place you are, only on the other side of the fire," Delia said. "Tempie will take the first hour's watch."

Tempest lowered her eyebrows, but she didn't argue. Even though she was tired, she could stay awake another hour, and she'd rather have her sleep all in one block. Besides, she'd vowed after worrying with the packhorse all day that she'd wake up earlier than usual the next morning and get her things ready to move out. Fairlee could have the packhorse the next day.

"We can stand watch," Tyrell said.

"Yes, you can and will for your hour. We aren't nuns anymore. We'll pull our own weight," Delia told them. "I'd like the last watch, if that's all right with everyone. In return, I will make breakfast and have it ready when you awake."

"That sounds fair enough to me," Isaac said.

Tyrell wondered if she had an ulterior motive, but he was too tired to reason it out. "I'll relieve Tempest and do the second watch. Isaac can follow me, and Micah will follow him. Fairlee can have the one just before Delia," he said.

Isaac and Micah nodded in agreement.

58

Micah stoked up the fire. "Remember to keep it burning during your watch," he reminded Tempest.

"You don't have to tell me what to do. I'm nineteen years old, and this is not my first time to travel like this," she said.

"Don't get all thorny with me, lady," Micah said coldly.

"Don't get all bossy with me," she told him.

Tyrell would have smiled, but it would have used too much energy. He left the pair glowering at each other and went to toss out his bedroll. He looked forward to a nap before Tempest awoke him for his watch.

Tyrell had been asleep when Delia brushed out her hair and braided it into two long black ropes before she went to sleep, but during his watch he stared at her as long as he wanted without the guilt he had felt when she was a nun. She was a lovely lady, and, by golly, she'd kept up all day without whining. Even if he didn't take to women who didn't know their place, he had to admire her and her sisters. Traveling with them wouldn't be nearly the burden he had thought it might.

His hour nap had spoiled him for sleeping after his watch, so he kept the fire going for one more. By that time he was yawning. He awoke Isaac and handed him the watch but still had a hard time turning off the images of Delia Lavalle looking so fragile as she slept.

"Huh," he grunted. *A rattlesnake looks peaceful when it's all coiled up in the sunlight. Poke it, though, and it'll strike you dead. Those women might be just as poisonous, Tyrell Fannin, so keep your distance. Do your job, and go home to your cotton fields.*

Hours later he awoke to the aroma of something frying. He threw back the blanket and pulled on his boots. Delia was at the fire, bending over a skillet. Tempest was busy getting the supplies back onto the packhorse. Fairlee was just rolling out of her blankets.

Tyrell held his hands up to warm them at the fire. "What's cooking?"

"Rabbit. Caught two on my watch, so we're having them for breakfast," Delia said.

"I didn't hear shots," he said.

"That would have been a waste of ammunition. They were close enough that I used my knife."

"You stabbed them? What did you do, mesmerize them into standing still?" Tyrell asked incredulously.

"She's not a witch," Tempest said. "She

60

threw her knife. She can hit a rabbit at twenty feet with her eyes closed. We'll have to leave the skins. That doesn't set too well with her, but they'd never travel all the way to Louisiana."

"We usually tan the hides for moccasins. They make nice warm ones for the cold months," Delia explained.

"Well, it smells good. I'm glad we all agreed you could have the last watch. I'm hungry." Tyrell was amazed that he could string entire sentences together.

"Better wake up your sleepy cousins, then. And, Fairlee, you get the supply horse today. Tempie's got hers saddled up and ready," Delia said.

Fairlee shot her sister a dirty look. "That's not fair. She got up early."

"Evidently she values riding without the extra horse more than sleep." Delia forked the pieces of browned rabbit onto a tin plate and set it near the fire, then dropped dough into the grease to make fry bread. It was already puffing up when she slapped the lid onto the skillet. In a few minutes she opened it up and turned each biscuit so they'd be brown on both sides.

When they were done, she put them onto a separate plate and set them beside the rabbit. Breakfast was ready. Delia was hungry, and her horse was saddled to go. She sat down on a fallen log, peeled the meat from the haunch of a rabbit, and stuffed it inside the bread. It wasn't bacon or even good seasoned sausage, but it would keep body and soul intact for a long ride.

Tempest echoed her sister's thoughts. "Reckon we might turn this into bacon if we think about it hard enough?"

"Jesus turned water into wine," Fairlee said.

"I don't think Jesus is going to turn rabbit into hog," Tyrell said wryly.

"Why not? He can do miracles. Not just anyone can turn water into wine," Delia argued.

"I think he worked a reverse miracle with you women. He turned wine into water," Tyrell said.

Isaac chuckled at the joke.

Micah frowned for a moment before he got it, and then he laughed aloud, "He sure did, didn't he? Went right from the sacred to the profane. From Sisters to sisters."

It took Delia a minute to understand his humor, but when she did, she smiled.

Tyrell's heart stopped beating. Never had he seen a woman so beautiful as Delia Lavalle with a smile on her face and amusement in her light blue eyes.

"I guess he did, didn't he?" she said. "We started out as holy women and got turned into plain old gals without halos or big fluffy angel wings either."

Tempest packed a biscuit with meat and bit into it. "It does taste a little like bacon. And let me tell you something, Mr. Fannin. If you've got a lick of sense, you'd rather have water with you than wine."

His brown eyebrows shot upward. "Oh?"

"Yes, sir. Holy women in a wagon were holding you back. We water women can get us all home a lot quicker," she said.

Tyrell reached for his second biscuit. "I will concede that point to you, Miss Lavalle."

"It's not much to concede. Right is right, no matter how you look at it. We might've been 'wine' before in that nuns' garb, but water will save your life more than wine. Now finish your breakfast. We've got miles to ride, and I'm eager to get home," Tempest said.

Delia cleaned her skillet and the plates with sand and stuffed them into the sack tied onto the packhorse. She kicked dirt onto the fire until it died, extinguishing all the embers. Wildfires were always a threat, and in a place without water, the damage could be formidable.

While everyone else finished eating, she sat down with her back to the tree and unbraided her hair, combed it out, and piled it on top of her head, pinning it securely before settling her hat over the bun.

Tyrell watched the whole process from a distance as he put the blanket and saddle onto his horse. He and the horse had been together for six years, and they understood each other. When his hand slipped and he almost dropped the saddle, the horse remained perfectly still. Then he cinched it almost too tightly, and the horse barely made a protest.

"Sorry about that, old boy," Tyrell whispered. "Better keep my mind on what I'm doing."

The sun should have been rising by the time they rode out, but clouds covered it, and a chilly wind blew down from the north. Delia turned up the collar of her duster and pulled her hat lower on her head, tying the strings tightly so it wouldn't blow away. They crossed the Yegua Creek sometime around noon and stopped to water the horses and refill their canteens. They chewed on beef jerky that she pulled from the saddlebags and moved on. A flash of lightning danced around on the prairie, and a violent burst of thunder spooked the horses, but with a few gentle pats and some sweet talk, they kept moving. Less than a mile later the rain began, not as a gentle mist but a downpour that gave them only a few feet of visibility.

There was no sense in stopping to make camp. There would be no dry wood for a fire, and the rain would put one out if they got it started, so they kept riding.

Delia could have fallen to the ground and kissed it when they saw lights in the distance and a hand-painted sign pointing north that indicated that Yellow Prairie was a mile ahead. They rode into the town at nine o'clock that night, a ragged bunch of wet travelers, even more tired than they'd been the day before.

Tyrell tethered his horse at an inn and came out shaking his head. "No rooms. All filled up. Y'all got a problem sleeping above a saloon?"

Delia shook her head. She'd sleep in a broom closet with rats right then, and she hated rats worse than rattlesnakes.

Tyrell crossed the road to a building that had a swinging sign with YELLOW PRAIRIE SALOON written in fancy scroll on it. Piano music floated out and competed for attention with the rumble of distant thunder.

He returned in a few minutes and remounted. "Livery is down the road a piece. We can board the horses there and get them fed and watered. The saloon man has three rooms. I took them all. You women can share, can't you?" He had to yell over the wind and rain.

Delia nodded. If it was dry, she'd sleep on the floor. She'd almost commit murder for a night's rest and a good plate of food the next morning she didn't have to cook. Right then she was too exhausted even to chew and swallow.

The owner of the livery stable assured them he would take good care of their animals and they'd have nice, dry stalls for the night. Delia and her sisters each removed what they needed from their saddlebags and tucked it up under their coats. They followed Tyrell back to the saloon and ignored the stares of the few men who were still drinking as they went up the stairs to the rooms.

Delia opened the door to number two with a big skeleton key. Two double beds, one on either side of the room. The bedsteads were wooden, and the sheets looked clean. Quilts were folded on a dresser between the beds.

She peeled off her coat and hung it on a nail on the wall. Fairlee and Tempest followed her example. Next they lined up their wet boots against the wall and then hung their wet clothing on extra nails pounded into the rough planks. After that they stripped down and rubbed their bodies dry with the smallest quilt from the stack, then donned clean undergarments and crawled between the sheets.

Fairlee and Delia shared a bed. Tempest kicked and talked in her sleep, so neither sister would sleep with her except in dire circumstances. Within seconds both of the younger girls were snoring softly, like purring cats. Delia sighed. Her stomach growled, but food would have nauseated her in her present state of physical exhaustion. She wondered if Tyrell had gotten the third room to himself, with the other two men sharing one.

Anger rose up in her. Why should Tyrell Fannin have a room all to himself? That wasn't one dang bit fair.

The mad spell didn't last long. Neither anger nor the piano music and noise from the first floor could keep her awake for long.

CHAPTER FOUR

Delia awoke at her usual time, long before daybreak. Grateful that her clothing had dried, she dressed quietly, leaving her sisters to rest a while longer. No aromas of frying ham or bacon drifted up the stairs, and the room below the bedrooms proved empty except for one woman sitting in front of the piano.

"Good morning," Delia said.

The lady turned. A beautiful girl with flowing red hair and even white teeth, she couldn't have been more than seventeen. "Who are you?" she asked.

"Just one of six travelers who needed a place to sleep last night. The hotel was full and suggested there might be rooms here," Delia said.

"I'm Scarlet, and I play the piano here," the girl said quickly.

"I'm Delia, and my sisters and I are on our way home to Louisiana. We were in San

Antonio, and our father thought it would be too dangerous for us to stay."

"Heard they've got the mission cut off. Been that way for more than a week now. They say Santa Anna has so many men that they look like ants crawlin' over the country-side. I heard tell that he's sly as a fox and meaner'n a rattlesnake," Scarlet said.

The room seemed to spin for a moment, but Delia got control of the light-headedness and blamed it on a lack of supper the night before. Her father would survive. Even if the mission was lost to Santa Anna, Captain Robert Lavalle wouldn't be killed. He would escape death to come back with more men and kill Santa Anna, she assured herself.

Delia took a weathered chair off a table and sat down. "Are you sure? Where did you get your information?"

"Comanche. One came through last night with news from the south. He had a drink and didn't stick around too long, but then, they don't. Harlin is one of the few in the area who'll sell to them. He'd sell whiskey to a hog if the critter could put money on the bar," Scarlett whispered.

"Harlin doesn't sound like a very pleasant man," Delia said.

"He isn't, but he pays me good, and Momma needs the money. Pa died last year, and she sews for money, but it don't stretch far enough, so I work here. Harlin is a rat, but he leaves me alone 'cause my playin' brings in the customers," she said.

"Where would one find breakfast in this town?" Delia asked.

"Over at the hotel. You don't have to stay there to eat there. Don't order the flapjacks. That Mabel tries to make them without using enough eggs and soda. It's like chewin' on jerky," Scarlet said.

"Thanks for the tip. You have a nice day," Delia said as she made her way to the door.

Tyrell had stopped at the top of the steps when he saw Delia talking to the bar girl. He couldn't hear a word of what the women said, but Delia's body language said she was comfortable talking to the red-haired girl. Most well-bred women would have shunned a piano player in a saloon.

He was finding more and more to admire about Delia Lavalle, and none of it made him feel a bit better. She might be a good person and a woman who'd do to ride across rough country with, but she was too danged headstrong for Tyrell.

When Delia started to leave the bar, he called out, "Where are you going?"

She stopped so fast, her forward momentum almost sent her into a facedown fall.

"To eat," she said simply.

He crossed the room in a few long, easy strides. "And where would that be?"

"The hotel. Miss Scarlet tells me they'll sell us breakfast even if we don't sleep there," Delia said.

"I'll join you," Tyrell said.

"Are you sure you can endure eating with someone who duped you?"

"I'll give it my best shot," Tyrell said.

Lord, tell me what to do to make him angry, Delia prayed silently. Tyrell Fannin was impossibly handsome even when he was scowling. When he smiled, as he was doing now, he could charm the eyelashes off a bullfrog. Delia was determined not to like the outlaw. Her father would never accept someone he'd had to bail out of jail as a match for one of his daughters.

She shrugged with feigned indifference, and he walked along beside her. The morning air was crisp, and the rain had left its fresh scent lingering behind. Water filled the potholes in the street. The children of Yellow Prairie would have a great time playing in the mud that day, and their mothers would carp about having to get their clothing clean again on laundry day.

Delia carefully stepped around the muddiest areas and wiped her feet on the rag rug on the porch in front of the hotel. Tyrell politely opened the door for her, and she was met with the wonderful smell of cooking.

Tyrell put a hand on the small of her back to lead her to a table. Fire jumped from his fingertips through her shirt to her bare skin. She was sure she'd have a mark there that would last for days. Hunger, she decided, was affecting her altogether differently than it usually did. Most of the time she got meaner than an old boar hog. That morning it flushed her face and made her light-headed.

A short, skinny woman with a chiseled face and slicked-back brown hair was beside the table the moment they were seated. "What'll y'all have this mornin'?" she asked.

"Bacon, and lots of it. Fried eggs and biscuits. Fried potatoes if you have them, and a cup of black coffee," Delia said.

Tyrell looked at a pint jar filled with honey and one with syrup sitting on the table. "You got flapjacks?"

The woman nodded.

"I'll have all of what she just said and a stack this big of flapjacks." He stretched his thumb and middle finger as far as they would go.

Six inches of flapjacks that would be as

tough as jerky, according to Scarlet. Delia smiled inwardly but didn't say a word about the flapjacks, but she did tell Tyrell what Scarlet had heard from the Indian the day before.

"So you did get out just in time. The place is under siege, and Santa Anna is planning to starve the Texans out," Tyrell said.

Delia tilted her chin up. "My father is a seasoned soldier. He'll fight to the end, escape capture, and return with another army and defeat Santa Anna."

Tyrell looked out the window thoughtfully rather than make a comment. The Alamo would fall from the sheer numbers Santa Anna brought with him. The Texans were mean and ferocious as cornered rats, but even a fighting rat wouldn't have a chance with a dozen hungry cats surrounding it. Santa Anna and the Mexicans were fighting to keep their land. The Texans were fighting for independence. Both had good soldiers. Santa Anna just had more of those good soldiers than Captain William Travis and Jim Bowie, Davy Crockett and Captain Robert Lavalle.

All he'd heard while he was in the jail was that the Alamo could protect the Texans, and from the fortress they would slaughter all the men Santa Anna wanted to spare.

73

But reality told a different story, and the Alamo *would* fall. Whether or not Captain Lavalle survived was another matter. He'd trained his daughters well; he might walk away without a scratch. But then again, he could be the first one to die when all those Mexicans started over the walls. He hoped for Delia's sake that she was right.

The lady brought their coffee and set the pot in the middle of the table. "Y'all goin' north or south?"

"Northeast. We're headed to northern Louisiana," Delia said. She liked strong coffee, but what she'd just sipped would blister paint on a barn.

"Comanche country. Be careful. Never know if they're with the white man or agin him," she said. "It's more'n a day's ride to Wheelock, but if I was y'all, I'd make one day of it and go all the way there before I stopped. Never know about those Comanches. Might let you ride right through their camp without a word and never harm you. Then again, they might follow you and slaughter you in your sleep for your horses."

Goose bumps crawled up Delia's arms in spite of the long-sleeved shirt she wore. "What's in Wheelock?" she asked.

"They got a fort of sorts. Protection in times of raids. And they got a hotel that's

74

decent for you to sleep in — a little more protection than the open prairie. Them Comanches can see you comin', and they're a wily bunch. You won't see 'em until they're takin' the hair off your head."

"You been to Wheelock?" Tyrell asked.

"Come from there five years ago down to this place. My sister and her husband run the hotel up there. Someday I'm goin' back to see her, when things is settled more and Texas gets away from Mexico."

"Thanks for your advice," Delia said.

"It comes with the food." The woman smiled, and the sharp angles of her face softened.

She went back to the kitchen and in a few minutes brought out two plates loaded with vittles and a third one stacked high with pancakes.

Tyrell poured honey over the flapjacks and set them aside while he ate fried potatoes, bacon, and eggs with two biscuits. The bread wasn't nearly as light and fluffy as what Delia cooked, but it wasn't bad, and it went down well with the fried eggs.

Delia cut her bacon into small pieces and used it to top off her eggs. She was so hungry that even the stack of tough pancakes looked good, but by the time she finished everything on her plate, she was full.

Tyrell cut into the pancakes and rolled his eyes with the first bite.

Delia smiled wickedly.

"How did you know they weren't going to be good?" he asked accusingly.

"Saloon girls know a lot," she whispered from behind her hand.

"Why didn't you kick me under the table or something?" He chewed and chewed and chewed. Even Micah's griddle cakes weren't this tasteless and tough, and he thought those could choke a full-grown hog to death.

She raised one shoulder in a shrug.

Fairlee and Tempest, followed by Isaac and Micah, filed into the room. Their eyes lit up at the smell of bacon. They gathered chairs around the table where Delia and Tyrell were still sipping coffee and sat down.

"Pancakes!" Micah said.

The waitress appeared and took four orders, brought four more coffee cups, and set a jar of cutlery in the middle of the table.

Tyrell pushed his plate over to Micah. "Help yourself. My eyes were bigger than my stomach. You might as well finish them while you're waiting. I'm going down to the livery to pay our bill. We've got a long day ahead of us and Comanche territory to get through."

"I'll go with you." Delia stood up.

"Comanches?" Tempest shivered.

"We're going to a place called Wheelock, and it has a hotel. It'll be worth the long ride," Delia told her.

They'd barely made it to the door when they heard Micah say to Isaac, "Help me out here, brother. I can't eat this stack all by myself."

Grinning, Delia turned back to see the look on Isaac's face.

Isaac managed to chew a bite without killing his brother. He then pushed the plate of flapjacks to Tempest and handed her a fork from the jar in the middle of the table. "Help yourself," he said generously. "We'll share, just like gentlemen should."

Tempest took a bite but spit it into a napkin. "That was mean!" she declared.

"Not any meaner than you are most of the time," Isaac replied, chuckling.

Delia and Tyrell hurried out the door, with Micah and Isaac's laughter echoing off the dining-room walls.

The clouds that had covered the sky the day before had moved on, and the sun was the tip of an orange ball peeking up at the end of the world. With the driving rain forcing them ahead, Delia hadn't even noticed

77

that they'd entered prairie country. As she and Tyrell walked side by side toward the livery, she realized how little protection the land would offer them that day. For the first time she was grateful to have three strong men riding with her and her sisters. She glanced admiringly at Tyrell, then quickly turned her attention back to the day ahead.

She and Tyrell saddled the six horses and adjusted the packhorse's load. She worried that they'd have to leave the packhorse behind and make a run for it if the Comanches did try to chase them down for their mounts. She should probably take charge of it that day. If Tempest had it, she'd likely hang on to it with the tenaciousness of a momma mountain lion keeping her babies from danger, but in doing so she might get herself killed. Fairlee would get flustered and hesitate, trying to make a decision, and that could get *her* killed. It seemed that the only way to keep her sisters alive under possible attack was to keep the packhorse with her.

"I'll take the packhorse today."

"What's that, Miss Lavalle?" Tyrell asked.

"I wasn't talking to you, Mr. Fannin. I was talking to myself. Sometimes I work out problems that way."

"Is that so," he said wryly, shaking his

78

head as if to suggest she was a little bit loco.

"It is," she retorted. Her tone was frosty. Surely he wasn't going to carry a grudge all day about those stupid pancakes. If so, maybe she'd been wrong to be thankful that they had three strong men with them. Maybe all they had were two strong men and one pouting little boy.

Tyrell shrugged and went to pay the liveryman. The horses were well fed, watered, and rested. He didn't regret a penny he gave the man, but paying the hotel woman for those flapjacks wasn't going to be easy.

He led three horses out of the livery, and Delia controlled four. When they reached the front of the hotel, he draped the reins he held over a hitching rail and went inside. Tyrell paid the bill while the other four finished off their food and trooped out of the inn.

Fairlee groaned when she saw the horses all ready to go. "I suppose I'll have to take care of old tagalong there."

"No, I'm taking a turn with him today," Delia said. "Your slickers are in the saddlebags, but it doesn't look like rain today."

"I'm not looking forward to this ride, I'm here to tell you," Tempest said.

79

"Do I hear a whinin' woman?" Micah asked.

"What you heard was an honest one. We'll see tomorrow morning who's the last one up and ready to go," Tempest shot back at him.

Tyrell came out of the hotel with a sour look on his face. "Damn pancakes cost more than that plate of bacon and eggs."

"Worth every dime of it," Micah said with satisfaction.

"Why's that?" Tempie's nose wrinkled with her puzzlement.

Micah settled into his saddle. "Because now there's a worse pancake than the ones I make. Tyrell's always said that nothing in the world could be worse than one of my flapjacks. I keep trying to make them right, but they never work. Now when he opens his mouth, I'll remind him that he paid good money for some that were ten times worse than mine."

Delia smiled once more as she eased into her saddle. She set her hat just right on her head, tying it snugly under her chin, and followed Tyrell's lead, leading the packhorse behind her.

CHAPTER FIVE

Tyrell drew up the horse's reins and held up a hand. The other five riders lined up beside him on the slight rise and looked down at the Indian teepees. They covered the land all the way to where yellow prairie grass met the sky. The sun was straight up. They'd be riding into the Indian village in a half an hour, and it would take a good hour or more to ride through it.

"Do we go around or through?" Tyrell wondered aloud.

"What do you think?" Delia asked him.

"We've got no cover when we leave this hill, no matter which way we go. They're going to see us no matter what," Tyrell said.

"Then I say we show courage instead of fear and ride right through," she said. After all she and her sisters had endured the past year, she'd be danged if the Indians were going to scare her.

"Rest of you agree with that? It's your

pretty scalps at risk, too," Tyrell said.

A vision of an Indian brave with Delia's long black hair flowing from his belt sent a chill to his toes. If he was the cause of her being hurt, he'd never forgive himself.

Tempest figured she could outtalk anyone, Indians included, on the face of the earth, so she nodded.

Fairlee thought she could outride anyone, even if the Indians were noted for having fast ponies. If they were riding to kill her, she'd be riding for her life, and that would give her the advantage. She nodded.

Micah and Isaac didn't see much difference either way, so they both nodded.

Tyrell led the way. "Okay, we ride through and hope for the best. Keep your eyes open, and make a dash for it if arrows or bullets start to fly."

Delia followed him with Isaac, Fairlee, Tempest, and Micah in line behind her. They rode slowly instead of keeping up their speed. Speed would draw attention to them and might give the appearance of fear. If they rode along leisurely, they might make it to the other side without an incident.

Unfortunately, it didn't work out that way. They didn't even make it to the edge of the village before an entourage of Comanche rode out to meet them. Twelve Indians sat bareback on horses of every color and description — paints, roans, blacks, and mixtures of them all. They fanned out in a row to show strength, so Tyrell motioned for his group to do the same.

He nodded at the most decorated Comanche facing him. "We only want to go through your land to the other side. We are travelers, not warriors," he said.

The one he talked to looked at a young man beside him, who translated. The Indian spoke a few words, and the young man looked at the white people.

"You will follow us into the village, where Chief Running Deer will talk more," he said.

A dozen Comanche surrounded the white people and escorted them into the village, where they were taken to a large teepee. The Indian slid off his pony and went inside without looking back.

Tyrell waited.

"You will follow him. You and your people. All," the younger man said with a circular movement of his hand.

Tyrell took a deep breath and led the way into the teepee. The chief sat at the back on a stack of fur pelts. He motioned for them to sit.

"He says to sit and we will talk. I am White Wolf. I know your language."

"Tell Chief Running Deer that we honor him as the chief of these people and wish to do him no harm. We are on our way home from a long journey," Tyrell said.

Comanche words were spoken softly.

"He says you can all pass safely if he can have the woman with eyes like the sky," White Wolf said.

Tyrell jerked his head around to see Delia's face lose its color and go pale.

Tyrell looked Chief Running Deer in the eye. "Tell him this woman is my wife. I cannot use her to trade. Why would he want her, anyway? She's good for nothing. Burns the food when she cooks."

Delia opened her mouth to say something, but Tyrell gave her a brief, meaningful glance to silence her.

After words were exchanged, White Wolf turned back to Tyrell. "The woman is for his son. His son would like her blue eyes, and they might have children with blue eyes. They would be honored in our tribe."

Tyrell shook his head slowly. "None of us can give up our wives. I'm sorry. Can we give you something else as a gift of our gratitude for your hospitality?"

Delia was so upset that she could scarcely sit still. Tyrell's wife indeed! If they got through this scrape safely, she'd give him a piece of her mind that would scorch the hair out of his ears. She looked up to see if he had hair in his ears. Not a one.

Before White Wolf could finish the exchange, the tent flap opened, and a little white girl rushed inside. Chief Running Deer's face lost its stoniness, and he looked exasperated.

"They are hitting me again. Make them stop. I want my momma," the child whined. She had blue eyes and a tangled mess of blond hair hanging into her eyes. After one look at Delia, she ran to her side. "Make them stop hitting me. They don't like me because I'm different. I want to go home."

"Who is this child?" Delia asked.

"Women don't speak unless they are spoken to," White Wolf said brusquely. "Sky Eyes, go and find your father."

"He's not my father! I don't like him," she said, and she clung to Delia's arm.

"That is a white child," Tyrell said.

"We found her. Chief Running Deer gave her to his son. If he doesn't find a wife for his son, then this girl will be his wife when she is old enough. His son thinks the blue eyes will bring strength to our people. He saw it in his vision when he became a man."

Delia shivered and put her arms around the little girl.

"My wife likes the child. She cannot have a baby of her own. Ask Chief Running Deer if I could buy this child for my wife," Tyrell said.

The chief shook his head emphatically.

"He says that the child was a gift to his son. If he can buy the woman, then she can be the girl's mother in this village and will be protected," White Wolf said.

Tyrell ran his fingers through his hair. He could take two Lavalle sisters home or leave all three of them for dead. He made his decision. "Ask the chief if he would choose one of the other wives. This one is not for sale."

Tempest gasped. "You wouldn't dare!"

"Woman, be quiet," Micah said firmly.

Tempest shoved a finger into his face. "Don't you talk to me like that, you fool! I won't put up with it. I'm not a bag of sugar you can sell anytime you want to."

White Wolf grinned. "The chief says he doesn't want that one. She's too ornery."

Tyrell nodded at Fairlee.

Words were exchanged.

White Wolf shook his head and pointed at Delia.

"I'm meaner than Tempest is," Delia stated. "If you make me stay, I will kill your son in his sleep. I love my husband, and I'd rather be dead than have another." Delia looked Chief Running Deer right in the eye the whole time she talked.

White Wolf translated.

"Chief says he believes the woman. You did not do well when you got these three. You would have done better to come to the Comanche. We train our women better than the white man does," White Wolf said. "But he cannot let you ride across his land without something. It would not look good. His people would think that he was weak."

Delia hugged the little girl close to her side. "You'd better talk fast and hard, because I'm taking this child with us," she whispered to Tyrell.

"My wife wants this child. What would the chief trade her for?"

It took several minutes before White Wolf turned back to Tyrell. "He says the girl is worthless. She causes trouble. Your wife shouldn't want her. He will trade a nice Comanche girl for something."

Delia glared at him and held the girl even tighter. "This one is the only one I want. I have a rifle I will give him for her."

Chief Running Deer studied her for a long time before he rattled off something else.

"He says you can keep your gun. He wants the extra black horse and all the things you have tied to him," White Wolf said.

Negotiations had begun, and Delia wasn't about to pay the asking price — not at first, anyway. "Tell him he can have the supplies. There's food and good pans, but he cannot have my horse. It's a good horse, and this girl is just a small child."

She listened without taking her eyes from the chief as he thought about her offer.

He shook his head slowly.

"He says the horse, the supplies, *and* your gun for the girl. And safe passage through for that. It's the last deal he'll make, woman. And you are never to tell anyone that he dealt with a female. It would be a blow to his pride," White Wolf said.

"We will take his deal. My wife is honored to give him the gift of our packhorse and supplies, and she thanks him for the gift of this child," Tyrell said quickly.

"You may go now. We will escort you across our land, and you can take the child with you. The horse and your supplies and gun stay with Chief Running Deer," White Wolf said.

They walked out of the teepee, and Delia went to the packhorse to remove their slickers. White Wolf put a hand out and shook his head. "That is not the deal. You traded it all for the girl. Now go." He raised his voice, and immediately more than a dozen braves had surrounded them again.

White Wolf removed Delia's rifle from the leather case attached to her saddle. He saw that it was a fine gun, and the girl had been a bother from the day they'd kidnapped her. His chief had made a good trade.

Delia mounted her horse, and Tyrell handed the dirty child up to her. They rode out two by two, as if they were really couples, and the Indians rode around them in an eerie silence that frightened Delia more than the worst thunderstorm ever could. People came from their teepees to stare at the white people as they were escorted out from among them. Women gathered their children closely, as if the women with the light eyes would snatch one of them away.

One brave rode hard from the other side of the encampment toward them and stopped the whole parade. He gestured toward the child and made a fuss until one of the other braves made him understand what had transpired. Then he pointed at Delia and sent the young brave off to get the translator. The five minutes they waited was only a few seconds short of eternity to Delia. She worried that the brave, obviously the chief's son, might override his father's trade. Could he do that? Or would it bring some kind of Indian voodoo down upon him?

White Wolf rode the packhorse into the mix of whites and Comanche and hopped down. He showed the brave what a fine horse it was and told him about the supplies and the guns, reminding him that white children as well as white women would always be there for the taking. They could grab another blue-eyed female, but good horses and guns weren't so easy to come by.

Finally the one holding up their progress moved aside. He picked up the packhorse's reins and led it back toward his father's teepee. It would be his horse because he'd just lost two blue-eyed women.

"Go now. He is happy," White Wolf said.

"Well, thank God for that. We wouldn't want him to be upset," Delia muttered.

White Wolf frowned at her. "White women need to keep their silence. They will be the fall of the white man's world if they don't learn their place. Leave her with me, and I will teach her to be quiet. A strong, green switch is good to train a woman who speaks when she shouldn't."

"I'll take your advice and beat her when we get to our home," Tyrell said.

90

"You and what army?" Delia mumbled.

"Beat her hard, every day for a week. She will learn. She's not a stupid woman, even if she is useless for childbearing," White Wolf said.

"Why do you speak English?" Tyrell asked, then wished he could take the words back. They could be riding away right then instead of sitting and waiting for an answer.

"I was captured by the white man as a child and held for three summers before I escaped and found my way back to my people. I learned your speech. It has been a help to Chief Running Deer. Now you will go. Remember to beat your woman. She will learn to obey," he said.

Tyrell didn't say another word. *Beat Delia?* Now, that would be a feat he didn't want to try. It would be like trying to tame a mountain lion or, worse, a rattlesnake. The woman might lose a battle of strength, but she'd find a way to get even, and that was a scary thought.

An hour later they were on the backside of the village, and the Comanche split away with war whoops that made Delia's hair stand on end. They were left on their own, one horse less, one extra child.

"What is your name?" Delia asked her.

"I'm not Sky Eyes. I am Hannah Marie

91

Smith. One of those mean Indians put me on his horse and carried me away," she said.

"How old are you?" Delia asked as they picked up their speed.

"Six. Momma and Daddy were chasin' cows that got out. Momma said for me to stay in the house. I wanted to help, so I went outside and found one cow, but then the Indians came from behind the trees," she said.

"When was that?" Delia held her tightly and let the horse trot faster to keep up with Tyrell, who seemed hell-bent on getting away from the Indians. He probably had a devil of a sour taste in his mouth after all the lies he'd told. His wife, indeed! That would happen at the same time Lucifer put in an ice-skating pond in Hades.

"A long time ago. It wasn't even cold yet." Hannah snuggled down into Delia's embrace and yawned.

"Did they bring you a long way?"

"Not at first, but the camp has moved two times since then," Hannah said just before she fell asleep.

Tyrell slowed enough to ride beside her. "What are you going to do with that child?"

"Everywhere we go, I'm going to ask if anyone has lost a little girl. She knows her name, and she's old enough to recognize her parents. If we don't find them, I'll raise her myself," Delia said.

Tyrell rode on ahead. Despite her flaws, Delia Lavalle was a good woman. Too bad he didn't have space in his hardened heart for a good woman.

An hour later Tyrell called a halt. They'd reached the Brazos, and Tyrell remembered a ferry he and the boys had used when they were chasing the horse thief who'd killed Mr. Burnet. It couldn't be far, because he remembered a nearby town called Mumford, and the sign in front of him, pointing across the river, had MUMFORD written on it. He rode more slowly down the river for a mile until he found the ferry.

"Only take three of you at a time," the man said when they rode up.

"Isaac, Tempest, and Fairlee will go first," Tyrell said.

"Why?" Fairlee asked.

"Because I said so," Tyrell said curtly.

"Don't be hateful with her because you're angry at the Indians," Delia told him.

"Indians? Y'all come through Comanches? How'd you keep your hair?" the boatman asked.

"We traded a good horse and gun for it," Delia answered.

"You're a lucky bunch. They're nervous

right now. I keep to the other side of the river at night. They've been gatherin' down there — more and more comin' in. I heard that several tribes are unitin' for a raid." He talked as he led three horses and riders onto his ferry, collected the money from Tyrell, and shoved off. "Be back soon as I can. Keep your head low. They mighta follered you. Never can tell about them people. They live diff'rent than us white folks."

The Brazos was wide, but at least it was calm that day. The storm the day before would have had them sitting out the weather beside the river rather than having a ferry to take them to the other side.

Hannah awoke and whimpered. "I'm hungry."

"It'll be a spell before we can find food. You'll have to be a good girl. When we get to Wheelock, I promise you can eat all you want," Delia said.

"And candy? May I have a stick of candy?"

"If you're brave and don't cry," Delia said.

Hannah rubbed her eyes and wiggled. "I want to get down. I have to go behind a bush."

Delia went with her and lifted her ragged dress to help her with her equally worn undergarment. She flinched when she saw the stripes on her legs — some purple, some

94

yellow, others red and fresh.

"Why did the chief's son whip you?" she asked Hannah.

"He didn't. The kids did. They'd hold me down and raise my dress and use a switch on me. They said it would make me an Indian. I ran and ran, but they hit me anyway," she said.

Delia was glad they'd chosen to go through the village and that she'd given away the horse for the girl. Horses could be replaced. But eventually young Hannah's spirit would have been broken, and she'd be a misfit in a world she hadn't been born into.

"It's over now," she said as she helped Hannah put things aright. "Have you had a bath lately?"

"Not in a long time," she said.

"We'll have one of those too. I'll order a big tub, and we'll get you and your hair all clean. Then you'll need riding clothes and shoes." She looked down at Hannah's bare feet; she had so much dirt under her chipped toenails that they were nearly black.

"I'd like that," Hannah said shyly.

The ferryman had just returned when she and Hannah came out of the bushes. Tyrell and Micah were headed toward them and looked worried.

95

"What took you so long?" Tyrell asked.

"Girls take longer than boys," she said.

"Y'all ready to get across? Ride them animals on down here!" the boatman yelled.

They were on the other side with the rest of the party in half an hour. The sun had long since begun its journey toward setting in the west, and they'd lost a lot of time that day. It would be well past dark before they reached Wheelock. Tyrell pulled a bag of jerky from his saddlebag and shared with everyone, including little Hannah. She chewed on it happily until the motion of the ride put her back to sleep.

At ten o'clock they rode into a quiet town. Tyrell went into the hotel and came back with two keys on big rings with numbers attached. "They only had two rooms left. They'll have to do. The innkeeper said there was food left from supper, and he'll put together a platter of cold meat and cheese for us."

"I'm almost too tired to eat." Tempest's tone betrayed her exhaustion.

"Hey, I thought you could tear up a mountain lion with your teeth." Micah's voice was edgy, but it too held weary undertones.

"Not after what we've been through today. I'm just grateful for four walls and a bed."

Tyrell remounted and pointed to the left. "Livery is this way. Food'll be ready when we return."

Hannah awoke and ate well, shoving food into her mouth with no table manners at all. She tucked a biscuit and a piece of cheese into her pocket when she thought no one was looking.

"Is it too late to get a tub of water?" Delia asked the innkeeper.

"Yes, ma'am. But that child is an unholy mess. I'll gladly fix a tub in the kitchen if you want to bathe her. How'd you let her get so dirty and ragged?"

"I didn't. The Comanche had her. We rescued her today. I'd like to bathe her before we put her into your sheets," she said.

"I'll get a small tub ready, and my wife can rummage around to find her something to sleep in tonight. Dry-goods store will be open in the morning. I'd burn them clothes she's wearing," he said.

"Good idea," Delia said.

"Do we have to wait until Hannah has her bath before we turn in?" Tempest asked after she'd eaten.

"No, you two go on up and get into bed. I'll be up shortly," Delia told them.

"I'll stay down here with you," Tyrell said.

"No need."

"Never know what might happen," he said. "I promised your father I'd get you home safely. Until you're secure in your room with the door locked, I couldn't sleep anyway."

"Thank you," she said softly.

"Did it hurt so much to say that?" he asked quietly.

"Yes, it did, but thanks anyway."

She stripped Hannah down to nothing, then faced a struggle when she started to toss her dress into the stove.

"No, no, no!" Hannah screamed.

"It's filthy and worn. It can't be fixed." Delia tried to reason with her.

Hannah snatched it and removed the hidden biscuit and cheese. Having rescued her stash, she laid it on the table beside the washtub that had been filled with warm water.

Delia lifted her into the water and picked up the bar of soap the innkeeper had left along with a drying sheet. She scrubbed the child and washed her hair vigorously. Then she picked up her bag and removed a comb. Half an hour later the knots were removed from Hannah's hair, and it hung in two long braids down her back. The white nightshirt she slipped over Hannah's head hung all the way to the floor.

"I feel so pretty now," Hannah said.

Delia touched her face. "You are pretty. You have freckles across your nose. They're cute."

Hannah reached up and touched Delia's chin. "You're pretty too. My momma has eyes like yours."

"You remember your momma pretty well?" Delia asked.

Hannah nodded. "And my daddy too. Momma has blue eyes like you do."

"Maybe we'll find your momma soon. Would you like that?"

A single tear sprang from Hannah's eye and traveled down her cheek as she nodded.

Delia's nerves were raw, but she held back the tears. "Ready for bed now?"

"Can the big man carry me? That one who fights with you?"

"Yes, he can," Delia sighed.

As tired as she was, she'd wondered how she was going to carry the child up the stairs. It was well past eleven o'clock, and tomorrow would bring another hard day of riding. She opened the door into the dining room to find Tyrell nodding off in a chair.

"Our princess would like for you to carry her up to bed," Delia said.

Tyrell looked down at the clean little girl.

99

"Why do you want me to carry you to bed?" He picked Hannah up and inhaled the sweet scent of a clean child.

"You're tall like my daddy. He carried me to bed every night. I'm 'tending," she said.

Tyrell looked at Delia, a question on his face.

Pretending, she mouthed silently.

Hannah laid her head on Tyrell's shoulder as they all trooped upstairs. His heart went out to her parents, wherever they were. To lose a daughter like that would tear his soul out of his body.

Delia unlocked the door and reached out. "I'll take her now."

"The dry-goods store won't open until after daybreak. Sleep a while in the morning. We've made good time. We'll get a late start," he said.

Delia took Hannah from his arms. Their fingertips brushed, and sparks seemed to light up the hallway. Delia figured the impression was due to bone-weary nerves. Tyrell refused to even think about it.

By the time Delia had Hannah tucked in, the child's eyelids were fluttering. She snuggled in next to Fairlee. Tempest was curled up in a ball in the bed on the other side of the room. Delia dropped her clothing and picked up the cloth hanging on the bar across the back of the washstand. She poured fresh water into the basin and wiped what seemed like ten years worth of dirt and worry from her face. If every day was like today, adding at least a decade to her age, she'd be an old, old woman by the time she got home.

She replayed the day's events as she washed the grime from her body. She'd been a "wife" for a little while and now a mother substitute, and she wasn't sure what she thought of all that. Especially if being Tyrell Fannin's "wife" meant keeping her silence unless spoken to. And the day any man — white, black, red — thought he could whip her would be a very cold day in hell.

CHAPTER SIX

Tempest sat straight up in bed and blinked several times. She looked around and sighed. She wasn't at home after all, as she'd been in her dreams. But it was daylight, and the sun was bright, filtering through the window and across the beds. Fairlee and Delia slept in the other bed, Hannah between them. Tempest eased out of bed and looked down at the little girl. Cleaned up, she looked even more as if she could actually be Delia's daughter, with her long lashes and delicate features. Her blond hair was the major difference, but that could be credited to a fair-haired father. In a couple of years everyone in Louisiana would forget that Delia hadn't actually given birth to the girl.

And that was the very worst thing that could happen. Delia was already twenty-one years old, bordering on being an old maid. She'd passed up several good suitors, and they were getting fewer and farther between. Tempest and Fairlee didn't figure they should marry before their older sister, and Tempest was feeling her age creep up on her. When they got home, she intended to make a more determined effort to find a suitable mate for Delia before Delia settled into the role of mother and forgot all about a husband!

The uncomfortable feeling of being stared at awakened Delia, and for a moment she, too, wondered why she was still in bed when the sun was already up. Then she remembered Tyrell's saying they'd need to wait for the store to open to purchase things for Hannah. Also she'd been physically and mentally exhausted the night before.

Tempest sat down on the foot of Delia's bed. "I was so scared yesterday, I thought I would die on the spot. Why did you keep arguing with that old Indian? It's a wonder he didn't have those braves kill us right there."

"Did you ever see so many bare chests in your life?" Fairlee asked from the other side of the bed as she woke up and got in on the latter part of Tempest's sentence. "That got my attention right quick. Anyone tough enough to ride around with no shirt in March wouldn't think twice about killing us for our scalps and horses. I'm glad you got Hannah out of there. Why are we sleeping in so late?"

"Store doesn't open until at least seven. I kept arguing with the chief because I didn't want that little girl abused anymore. I could tell by the way he looked at her, he wished he hadn't brought her into his family. The rest was just reaching an agreement that would make him look big and important. Indian men and white men aren't so very different," Delia explained.

Tempest laughed softly. "I guess we won't talk about the way Tyrell Fannin looks at *you*."

Fairlee smiled. "Wonder what we'll have to give him to take *you* away."

"I'm not nearly rested enough for teasing this morning," Delia said.

"Who's teasing?" Fairlee asked.

"You both had better be. Now, get up and get dressed. After breakfast we're going to the store. I'm buying supplies, and I hope someone has a mule or a horse for sale in this town. We won't be so lucky as to find hotels every night."

Delia had successfully changed the subject. Tyrell Fannin didn't look at her any differently than he did her sisters, she assured herself. They were no more and no less than a paying job to him. Whatever Tempest had read in his face was merely his desire to finish that job and forget about it and them.

She threw off her nightshirt and dressed in the clothing she'd worn for nine days. At least it wasn't summertime, or she wouldn't be able to bear the smell by now. She redid her hair before she awakened Hannah, who opened her eyes slowly and, without moving her head, scanned the room and the three sisters.

"Where am I?" the girl asked.

Delia explained the whole thing to her in a few short sentences.

"I need to go to the bushes," Hannah said.

"Not the bushes anymore. There's a chamberpot under the bed. Do you remember those?" Tempest said.

Hannah nodded and threw back the covers. "At my real home."

When she finished, Fairlee combed out her hair and braided it again. "Your hair is a little bit curly, like mine. The braids will keep it from flying around your face while we travel."

"Moving again," Hannah sighed.

"I'm afraid so," Delia said. "You'll be good and not cry?"

Hannah looked up. "You won't hit me?"

"Of course not. I don't hit little girls. I just want you to be brave. We'll go to the store and buy you clothing to ride in and some supplies so you won't get hungry again," Delia said.

"Like yours. Can I have boy clothes too?"

"Yes, you can," Tempest said. "When a girl does a boy's job, she gets to wear boy clothes, and riding all day long is usually a boy's job."

"A girl's job is cooking and washing clothes in the big pot," Hannah said seriously.

"That's right. When we get home that will be the girl job. But now we have to ride all day like boys so we can dress like them. Let's go have breakfast and then go to the store," Delia explained.

They marched down the stairs into the dining room to find Tyrell, Isaac, and Micah already sitting at a table. The plates before them were still half full, so they hadn't been up very long either. They stood when the ladies got to the table, and Tyrell pulled a fourth chair from an empty table next to theirs.

Delia made a conscious effort to notice the way he looked at her. Just as she'd suspected, it wasn't any different from the way he glanced at either of her sisters.

Oddly, she was a little disappointed.

His shirt bore a few stains, but it didn't look too horrid, considering that he'd worn it for more than a week. He was a very handsome man, his face now freshly shaven. She wondered why he wasn't married. Or was he? Was there a Mrs. Fannin or a prospective Mrs. Fannin waiting for him in Mississippi? The idea of either made her grumpy, and the fact that she even wondered or cared made her angry.

"Are you wanting to replace the pack-horse?" he asked Delia.

"Yes, I am," she said.

"While you're at the store, I'll check the livery and see if there's anything there for sale. You'll want something that can keep up the pace," he said.

The innkeeper's wife appeared with a fresh pot of coffee and set it in the middle of the table. "What will you ladies have this morning?" she asked. Her slight sneer and her flared nostrils gave away that she didn't really consider them *ladies* at all in their mannish trousers.

"Whatever they're having is fine," Delia said.

"For me too," Tempest and Fairlee said at the same time.

"And your daughter?"

"I want pancakes," Hannah said, loud and clear.

Delia looked at Tyrell.

"Delicious," he confirmed with a wink as he put the last bite into his mouth.

"Please bring her a glass of milk and add a few pieces of either bacon or sausage to her plate. Pancakes will fill her up, but long before dinnertime she'll be hungry again," Delia said, oddly warmed by Tyrell's wink.

"She's a sour-looking woman," Tempest whispered when their server had gone back to the kitchen.

"Shh, she'll hear you," Micah hissed.

"She was fine to us," Isaac said. "Laughing and talking and asking where we were going. Said there's nothing much up ahead for a few days but open prairie and buffalo."

"Some women don't take to others dressing like men," Tyrell pointed out.

Hannah piped up. "If a girl does a boy's job, then she wears boy clothes. I'm getting boy clothes today, too, because I'm going to ride a horse all day."

Tyrell chuckled deep in his chest.

"It's not funny." Hannah glared at him.

"One day with you Lavalle women, and she's already acting just like you," Tyrell said.

A couple came in the front door at that

moment. The woman carried a new cast-iron skillet back to the kitchen. The man stopped at the hotel desk and talked to the clerk behind it. They were on their way back out when Hannah looked up and hollered, "Momma!"

Delia put a hand on her shoulder and said, "Darlin', I'm not your momma. My name is Delia, remember. Now, what is it?"

Tempest smiled brightly. Maybe there was hope after all. Delia wasn't falling easily into the parent role, so there might be hope that she'd get married in the near future after all.

"No — Momma!" Hannah pointed and jumped up from her chair.

The departing woman stopped in her tracks and looked back. All the color left her face, and had the man with her not caught her as she fainted, she could have cracked her head on a nearby table.

"Hannah?" he gasped.

"Daddy!"

"Are those your parents?" Delia asked the little girl.

Hannah nodded but stayed still, as if she didn't know what to do next.

Tempest touched her arm. "Go on to them. It's all right."

Hannah ran across the floor. Her mother's

eyelids fluttered, and tears ran down her cheeks as she opened her arms. Hannah literally jumped into them from two feet away.

Her father looked at the party around the table and narrowed his eyes. "Why do you have our child?"

Fairlee was on her feet so fast that the chair she'd been sitting in crashed to the wooden floor, sounding like a clap of thunder. The noise brought the desk clerk from behind the counter and the cook from the kitchen. They'd never had a brawl in their dining room, but there was always a first time for everything, and those women were wearing men's clothing. No telling what other abominations they might create.

Fairlee crossed the room, talking and shaking her finger the whole time. "Don't you look at us accusingly, mister. We rescued your child from Indians just yesterday. I'm not sure how they snatched her, but my sister risked her life and gave up our pack-horse, our supplies, and her gun to get Hannah away from them."

"I'm so sorry," he apologized. "We'd given up on ever finding her. One minute she was in the house with her younger brothers. The next, she was gone. We had no idea what had happened to her."

110

"Apology accepted." Fairlee returned to the table.

"Hannah has been through a great deal," Delia said cautiously. "She was mistreated by some of the tribe's children because she looked so different from them. I'll show you." She turned the child around gently and pulled up the shirt.

Tears streamed down Mrs. Smith's cheeks when she saw the bruises. "Where was she?"

"About a day's ride south of here with the Comanche. She said they nabbed her in the winter and that they'd moved at least twice," Delia said.

"It wasn't winter, but it was late fall and cold when she went missing. Our cows got out, and we were chasing them back into the corral, and when we got back to the house, she was gone." Mrs. Smith teared up again and clutched her daughter to her as if she'd never let her go.

Mr. Smith cleared his throat. "I'm Morris Smith, and this is my wife, Allie Fay. We can never repay you for bringing Hannah Marie home to us, but we do have a good mule we'd be honored to give you to replace your packhorse."

"That's not —" Delia started.

Tyrell placed a hand on her arm and interrupted her. "We'd be glad to have it, sir,

111

and we're very happy that we've found Hannah's family. Delia Lavalle here and her sisters were going to look for you in every town we came across. It's fortunate that you all came in today."

"We operate the general store. Oh, my, Morris — the boys. We left them alone!" Allie Fay gasped.

"They're fine. The store is locked, and they're playing in the back room. Allie Fay's been spooked ever since Hannah went missing," he explained.

"She told us she only left the house to help you find the cows," Delia said.

"It doesn't matter now. She's home!" Allie Fay cried.

"That mule is down at the livery stable. I'll tell Gus that it's yours now. And thank you again." Morris picked Hannah up and carried her out the door with Allie Fay hugged up to his side.

The cook wiped at her eyes with the hem of her apron. "That was the sweetest thing that could ever happen. Your rooms and food are free. Don't even try to pay for them. We've all worried that Allie Fay would lose her mind over that child goin' missin'. This is a miracle!"

"Thank you," Tyrell said simply to the woman.

"Why did you do that?" Delia whispered angrily. "I could buy a mule or a horse, and those folks might need that one desperately."

"Because they needed to repay you. Be a good receiver as well as a good giver, Delia."

"Does that mean that we're wine instead of water today?" Tempie asked.

"Hardly. You ain't wearin' a habit, are you? Actually, I believe you gave 'em to the Indians," Isaac said.

At that Tempest started to laugh. "I can just see those big braves with those things on their heads."

The laughter was infectious.

When it died down, Isaac said, "Actually, they'll know what a nun's habit is because they've been around missions and white people. Wonder if they'll think they've brought bad luck down on their heads because they were dealing with the white man's holy women, not their wives."

"I hope they do," Fairlee said. "And I hope that superstition causes them to never take another white child from its parents."

The woman who brought their food didn't look at them with condemnation anymore. She pulled up a chair to hear the whole story about their encounter with the Indians. Later that day she'd be the queen in the gossip court as she relayed it to the rest of the women in town.

While they'd finished eating and telling the story, Tyrell and his cousins went to the livery to saddle up the horses and bring the mule around to the front of the store, where Delia and her sisters were planning to shop. When the women arrived from the hotel, all six horses were ready to ride.

Delia raised an eyebrow. "Well, well, you're helping us today?"

"Your good deeds paid for our rooms and breakfast," Tyrell said. "It's only fair."

"Would *you* have left Hannah in that Comanche village after seeing the way those other children treated her?" Delia asked.

"Probably," Micah offered. "There was no guarantee that we'd ever find her folks. They might've been killed, for all we knew. You were darn lucky," he added.

"Depends on how you define *lucky*," Delia told him as she marched resolutely into the store.

Allie Fay insisted that no money would exchange hands for the supplies Delia picked out. "I can't take your money, Miss Lavalle. As it is, I can never repay you for what you did. Hannah, come and say good-bye to these wonderful people."

Hannah came out from the back room wearing a calico dress with snow-white pantaloons showing at the hem. She wore stockings and new shoes. Her hair was still braided the way Fairlee had done it that morning, but it was very evident that she was Allie Fay's daughter when Delia saw them together. They shared all the same features. But Allie Fay was a petite woman, while Hannah had inherited her father's bone structure and would be a tall beauty someday.

Delia stooped down and slyly put a bag of money into Hannah's pinafore pocket. "When I'm gone, you take this out and give it to your mother," she whispered when she hugged the little girl. These hardworking people had already given her a mule; she couldn't, in good conscience, let them sacrifice even more of their livelihood.

"What is it?" Hannah whispered back.

"It's a surprise, and you get to give it to her, but you make very sure that we are out of town first, or it will be spoiled," Delia said.

Hannah stepped back and with a very serious look on her face said, "I wanted boy clothes but Momma said I'm doing girl work today so I have to wear girl clothes."

"Your momma is right. You listen to her and don't leave the house again when she tells you to stay inside," Delia said.

Hannah looked at Delia and swore, "I promise."

"Thank you," Allie Fay said. "For everything." Tears of joy and gratitude glistened in her eyes.

"Thank you for all you've done for *us*," Delia told her.

Allie Fay hugged all three of them. "I'll pray you have a safe journey home."

They all said their good-byes, then filed out of the store and mounted their horses.

Micah said he'd take care of the mule that day, since he'd be bringing up the rear, and the animal might need to adapt to walking all day. Truth be told, the man at the livery had told the men that the mule was a stubborn old creature and hated womenfolk. If they wanted the critter to keep up, they'd best keep the women away from him.

CHAPTER SEVEN

The sun was straight up when they came upon the Navasota River. Tyrell turned them toward the north, riding along on the western side of the river for another hour before he stopped to water and rest the horses. They wouldn't make twenty miles that day, but they'd traveled longer than that on others, so it would make up the difference. The morning he'd looked up and seen the Lavalle women without their habits, he'd still figured he was in for a long, slow trip. But they'd all three proved their mettle on the journey, and he seldom heard a sigh and never any whining.

There weren't many women who could stand up to such physical exertions and not a one who'd have looked Chief Running Deer in the face to negotiate with him. That Delia Lavalle was truly a piece of work. He wondered why she wasn't married — but not for long. The reason was obvious: most men probably couldn't stomach the notion of a wife who could outshoot and outride them. He chuckled quietly at the thought.

Everyone dismounted, but they left the saddles on the horses. Micah staked them out to graze on the green grass beside the river. The old mule had moved right along, but its head now drooped. It perked up considerably after a long drink from the river and went to chewing on the grass along with the horses.

Isaac gathered wood and started a small fire in the middle of the clearing.

Delia unloaded a new skillet and the ingredients to make a hoecake. She took out her precious jar of bacon drippings from her saddlebag and put a spoonful into the pan before she set it on the rocks Isaac had positioned around the fire for cooking. While that melted, she stirred up flour, soda, and water together, added a pinch of salt and three of sugar. When the skillet was hot, she poured the mixture in and put the lid on top. While the pan bread cooked, she unwrapped a thick chunk of cheese and some sausage Allie Fay had insisted they take along for dinner.

Tyrell walked up the river a few hundred yards and looked around. He checked the sky. No clouds. At least it wasn't going to rain and swell the river to keep them on the western side. The water was fairly clear and moving slowly. No white ripples, yet it looked too deep to cross without a ferry. His brow wrinkled as he tried to remember crossing it on the way to San Antonio. Who'd have thought Texas would have so many rivers? When he'd heard of the land west of Louisiana, he'd pictured it as desert — bone-dry and with no water — and wondered who in his right mind would want to live there.

Standing on the banks of the Navasota, he realized how easy it would be to love this land. Willow trees were starting to bud and waved their long branches in a soft breeze. Grass grew right up to the edge of the water. If they had these conditions — grass for the horses, water for drinking and washing — all the way to Louisiana, he'd be a happy man. Which reminded him — he hadn't washed his clothing in days. He had a spare set in his saddlebags but hadn't gotten them out without a place to wash what he was wearing.

Voices drifted down the river, carried by the breeze. He walked a little farther and saw a ferry. A dozen men on horseback were waiting their turns. He watched for a few minutes, then went back to the camp.

"About a mile upriver there's a ferry. Water is good. We could cross over and make camp there. Be nice to clean up our clothes and rest once we make the other side," he said.

"You sayin' we're dirty?" Tempest asked.

"I'm saying I am," Tyrell answered.

"I'd be for it," Isaac said.

"Delia?" Tyrell looked at her.

"Seems like a sound plan. Let's eat and douse the fire and move on," she agreed.

When they rode up to the ferry dock, the boatman was returning with no passengers. "I seen your fire up there and figured you'd be along soon. I can take three at a time. Don't make me no never mind how you divide it up."

"Better take Micah and Tempest and the mule first. Then Isaac and Fairlee and Delia. I'll wait until the end," Tyrell said.

Tyrell sat down on a fallen log and waited. He probably could have ridden his horse across and saved the money for the third fare, but that likely would have caused a stink with Delia. If he could ride the river, then she would have felt honor bound to try to do it also. Then again, it might have deflated her considerable ego to fall off her mount and have to swim to the other side in the cold water. He smiled at the image of her hat floating away and all that black hair flowing in the water when it escaped the pins.

"Where y'all headed?" the ferryman asked as he returned to take Tyrell and his horse across the calm river.

"Northeast. Up into Louisiana," Tyrell said.

"Ain't much between here and twenty miles up the road but open country. You want to stop for the night, I reckon y'all could use my barn. Won't charge you much, and you can keep your horses in there. Y'all can sleep in the loft. The missus don't cotton to me bringin' strangers into the house, but she don't got a problem with puttin' them up in the barn. It's down a ways from the house. Cows and horses are out in the pasture grazin' this time of year, so it's settin' empty," he said.

"We'd be obliged," Tyrell said. "Close enough to the river that we can do some washin' up?"

"It'd be a quarter of a mile down to the river, but there's a good well to the south of the barn. Draw up whatever you need. Use one of the waterin' troughs to wash if you want. No extree charge for that."

Tyrell thanked the man, and money exchanged hands for the ferry services and his barn. "Which way do we go?" Tyrell asked when they were on the other side.

"I'll lead the way. It ain't far. We built close enough to the river. Thought last spring when the river swelled that we mighta been downright crazy to do it, but it only got up as far as the back porch. Missus, she fished right off the porch. Got a couple of good-lookin' catfish, and we et on them for days."

"What's going on?" Delia asked when the man tied up the ferry and motioned for them to follow him.

Tyrell rode along beside her with Isaac and Tempest behind them and Fairlee and Micah bringing up the rear with the mule. "We're staying in his barn tonight. The horses will have a long, safe rest in the stables, and we can have the loft."

"Close to the river?" she asked.

"No, but there's a good water well and some troughs we can use to do laundry," Tyrell explained.

It was a far cry from a hotel with real beds, but Delia wasn't going to complain. Someday when she was an old woman, she'd look back at the experience and tell her grandchildren about the exciting adventure. Of course, right then it seemed more like an ordeal, and Aunt Rachel and Uncle

Jonathan were going to have apoplexies when they heard about it all.

The ferryman pointed at a barn sitting on the far side of a pecan grove before going into his house. "Y'all make yourselves to home. Be careful with a fire, and build it outside the barn. Hay is dry, and it'd be dangerous inside. There's an old chimney standin' not far down the hill back behind it. Old place was back here at one time. Heard the Comanches raided the place and scalped the folks. Ain't seen Indians in a few months, so you'll pro'ly be safe."

The barn was an old structure built on a stone foundation with wood that had weathered to a soft gray with age. It was nothing like the elaborate barns on the plantation where Delia and her sisters had been raised, but it beat sleeping with no shelter at all. Delia shivered whenever she thought of those strong Comanche braves, and the idea that they could possibly sneak up on them in the middle of the night out in the open was enough to give her nightmares until her dying day.

They built a fire in the stone chimney and heated water to put in a round watering trough Tyrell set in a stall of the barn. Isaac and Micah carried hot water until they had enough to warm the icy water they'd pulled

123

up from the well. Then, like gentlemen, they told the women they could have the first baths while they set about pulling up more buckets to heat for the second round.

Tempest unpacked her clothing from the saddlebags and carefully hung it over the side of the stall. She sat down in the warm water and thought that she'd never, ever take a simple bath for granted again. When the house servants drew water and carried it up all those stairs to the bathing room, she'd never given it a second thought. Now she'd at least remember to thank them.

When she finished, Fairlee got into the water and hurriedly bathed. She dried off with her dirty shirt and wished for one of the big white drying sheets that Rosy, the nanny who had taken care of all three Lavalle girls since they were born, wrapped her in after she'd bathed. Riding and hunting with their father might have prepared her for camping with no modern conveniences, but she sure didn't have to like it.

Delia was third to get into the water and didn't even care that it was lukewarm. She scrubbed hard. It might be a long time before they had another chance to bathe. If they rode as hard as they had been, it would always be too late to order up a bath in a hotel. They'd been on the road eleven days by then, and she figured it was twice that many more before they'd reach their destination.

A whole month with Tyrell Fannin and his Burnet cousins, she reflected. By then the men would probably be so glad to get rid of the Lavalle girls, they might start up another brawl in a saloon out of pure joy.

When she finished her bath, she and her sisters used the soapy water to wash their clothing. Tempest had brought back a bucket of cold, clean water to use for rinse water while Delia finished dressing. Tempest tied a rope to two nails in the barn walls and created a clothesline. They draped their wet things over the rope and hoped they dried by morning, when they'd have to pack them.

Leaving their undergarments hung out for the men to see was embarrassing, but there wasn't anything that could be done about it. Then the idea that Tyrell might hang his beside hers brought high color to Delia's cheeks.

It took all three men to dump the trough. Afterward they refilled it for their turns at a bath. Tyrell went first, and the cousins didn't argue.

"While they get cleaned up, we'll go ask the missus if she's got any supplies she might sell," Delia said.

"If there'd been travelers at Oak View, we would have *given* them supplies and put them up in something other than a barn," Tempest said crossly.

"Yes, but we're not at home. Oak View is a long way from here," Fairlee reminded her.

"I'll just be glad if they have anything they can sell. Especially milk," Delia said.

Delia knocked on the back door. Just as she decided that no one was about in the house and turned to leave, a woman with graying hair pulled back in a tight bun slung open the door and glared at then.

"What do you need?" she asked the girls bluntly.

"I was wondering if you might have some milk you could sell us and perhaps some meat for our supper," Delia said.

"Butter or sweet?"

"We'd prefer sweet milk, but we'd take buttermilk if that's what you've got," Delia said.

"I got both. Sell you both or either. Got a quarter of a side of bacon I could sell. Already smoked and seasoned, and we got an extree haunch of deer I cooked just this morning. Too much for the two of us. I reckon I'd sell it."

"We'll take it all and both jars of milk. We'll leave the jars on the porch tomorrow morning before we leave," Delia said.

"You wait here," the woman said without inviting them inside. "Women!" she muttered. "That's why Harry done let them stay in the barn. He's always had an eye for pretty girls. I'll have trouble with him wantin' to go out there," she grumbled loudly enough that they could overhear her.

Tempest clamped a hand over her mouth. "Guess we'd better set up a watch tonight after all," she whispered.

"I *thought* that old boatman talked too much and too fast. He kept lookin' at you, Delia, and it wasn't a good look, either. He might be more dangerous than the Indians." Fairlee kept her voice low also.

"Don't say a word to the men. They need their rest too. I'll take first watch," Delia said.

"Guess that's only fair. Harry wasn't lookin' at *them* like he could have them for breakfast," Fairlee said.

"He did look shifty, didn't he? I wonder if he lures weary travelers into his barn and then robs them. We'll have to be careful," Delia said.

"I think we should tell Tyrell," Tempest declared.

"No, not unless it becomes a problem."

The woman handed two gallons of milk out the door. "That'll be a dollar for all of it."

Delia dug into her pants pocket and brought out the money. The woman snatched it from her hand and went back for the bacon and venison.

"That's robbery," Tempest said.

"Just hope that they'll be satisfied with that and not try to really rob us," Delia said.

The woman returned. "Here. Don't be comin' back beggin' for no more. I ain't got nothin' else I intend to sell today."

"Yes, ma'am, and thank you," Delia said politely.

Tempest waited until they were halfway back to the barn before she exploded. "Beggin'? She accused us, the Lavalles, of beggin'? We have never begged in our lives. And we paid her twice what that would have cost in a store. Besides, if we'd have had someone stayin' in *our* barn, we would have *given* them more than that just to be good neighbors."

"Not everyone is a good Samaritan," Fairlee said.

"She never was 'wine' to begin with. She started out as branch water that would make a person sick if he even waded in it,"

Tempest fumed, "and she's stayed 'water.' "

"Now, Tempie. If you were married to that man of hers, you might be an old witch too," Delia said.

"No, if I was married to that man of hers, he'd be dead, and I'd be real nice," Tempie retorted smartly.

Delia and Fairlee both got a case of giggles, which brought on hiccups, which were funny too. Tempest couldn't stay mad with them laughing, so she joined in, and before they got back to the place where they'd cook supper, they'd all forgotten about the dollar the food had cost them.

Delia made biscuits and gravy to go with the venison. They had plenty of milk to drink with their supper, and she'd poured the buttermilk into two empty jars in her supply bag to carry with them for the next day's bread or for drinking. Either way, it would have to be used by the next night, or it would go bad.

"I'll take first watch," Tyrell said as the sun dropped below the horizon.

Delia jerked her head around to stare at him. "Why?"

"I'm not sleepy," he said, an edge in his voice.

"Besides, he didn't like the way that ferryman kept staring at you," Isaac said simply.

"I . . ." Delia started.

Fairlee nodded seriously. "And that woman up there that we bought the food from — she was muttering about Harry letting us stay here because he likes pretty women. I'll take second watch. Just wake me up."

"Fairlee!" Delia exclaimed.

"Well, she did, and Tyrell needs to know. I'm more afraid of that man than I was of the Indians. They were openly hostile. He's like a slimy old snake, just waiting under a rock to strike at us."

"We'll all be fine. We'll just watch out through the night and leave before first light. We've got enough food to eat on the trail. We won't even make a fire. Last watch should get the horses saddled and ready," Tyrell said.

"Keep your saddlebags under your heads for pillows. Harry might be out to do some stealing," Micah suggested.

"This is scaring me," Tempest said.

"Fear is unacceptable. Caution is necessary," Delia said.

"Those are Father's words," Fairlee said.

"Just remember them. Now let's get some sleep while we can," Delia said.

Everything went fine for the first part of the night. Tyrell took two hours' watch, then woke Micah, who took the next two. Micah was sitting in the shadows behind the ladder going up into the loft when Harry slipped into the barn. He went straight for the sacks that the mule carried and stole their coffee, shoving it into his shirt. He prowled around for saddles and saddlebags, but, finding none, he checked the clothing on the line.

He started up the ladder, then jumped as if he'd been shot when Micah cleared his throat.

"What can I do for you, Harry?" Micah asked.

Harry looked down at the gun in Micah's hand and stepped back down. "Thought I heard a noise. I feared them Indians might be prowlin' around. I was checkin' on you folks."

"We're all fine. We keep our own watch for Indians — and anyone else who might be out to do us harm," Micah said firmly.

"Well, I'll get on back to the house, then, if'n ever'one is safe," Harry said as he slipped out the door.

Micah awoke Isaac for the last watch and told his brother what had happened and to be careful. Isaac had the three men's horses saddled and ready when Harry made his second appearance.

"Y'all are up and about mighty early. Thought you might not be on the road until after breakfast," Harry said.

"Got miles to go and need to get home to our crops," Isaac said.

"You ready to pay me for the night, then?" Harry said.

"My brother gave you money for the barn and we've left things in good shape," Isaac said.

"He didn't pay me for the hay them horses et up or the rope y'all used for a clothesline. I told you to help yourself to the water, but I didn't say you could help yourself to my rope or my hay," Harry protested.

"Good morning," Tyrell said from the ladder coming out of the loft. "Everyone is up and ready to go. Thank you for the use of the barn. It served us well."

"You ready to pay me the rest of what you owe me?" Harry asked.

"He says we owe him for the hay our horses ate and the rope we used for our clothes," Isaac explained.

"Our women paid your wife for those things when they paid for the food and milk she sold them last night," Tyrell said.

Harry squinted. "The missus sold your women food?"

"Milk, bacon, and venison," Tyrell said.

"They paid her plenty to take care of whatever hay our horses might have eaten and the use of the rope. You about got those horses saddled, Isaac?"

Isaac was cinching up the last one by that time. "I sure do."

Tyrell called up the ladder. "Hey, y'all, we ride in two minutes."

The other four members of the party came down in a hurry and mounted up. They left Harry standing there with a blank look on his face.

"That went fairly well, don't you think?" Tyrell said when they were a mile down the road.

"There ought to be a sign put up a mile on either side of the ferry that lets folks know what kind of people Harry and the missus really are," Tempest said.

Tyrell chuckled. "Sounds like a good idea to me. Looks like with this early of a start, we'll make it to Val Verde before dark."

"Where?" Micah asked. Tempest's idea of a sign sounded fine to him. People like Harry shouldn't be allowed to take advantage of folks just because he owned and operated a ferry. Folks who weren't as smart and as alert as the Burnet brothers and the Lavalle sisters could be in big trouble.

"Remember that pretty little town we

stopped in on the way to San Antonio? The one where the lady flirted with Tyrell?" Isaac said.

Micah grinned. "Yeah, that schoolmarm tried to talk Tyrell into staying in Val Verde and not going on after James Durran for shootin' Pa in the back. She was a pretty little thing, with that blond hair and them big brown eyes. Looked like doe eyes, didn't they?"

Delia felt a flash of green that had nothing to do with the new, minty green leaves sprouting on the trees around them and everything to do with what felt suspiciously like jealousy.

CHAPTER EIGHT

Val Verde meant *green valley,* and the town was located in a lovely valley hedged by hills and surrounded by small streams. Everywhere Delia looked there were cedar and holly trees, some covered in brambles and vines of one sort or another. Even though it was only the first week in March, everything was already turning green. Whoever had named the village surely had named it well.

There was a school and a church, a blacksmith, and a general store. A sign swinging in the breeze announced that a doctor was in practice. But the sign Delia could have danced a jig in a pig trough over was for a hotel. It was a two-story clapboard building with an upstairs balcony. She didn't care if it had a dining room with a crystal chandelier from France or if the tables were rough wood with benches to sit on, as long as the beds were soft and the sheets clean.

"Reckon that schoolmarm will be in the

hotel eating supper again?" Micah teased Tyrell.

"I'm tired. I'm hungry. That's a bad combination for you to risk joshin' me," Tyrell said.

"You can get rested, and you can eat. Maybe she'll talk you into stayin' around a while, since we aren't chasin' the devil this time. Bet these womenfolk would like to be still a couple of days. They've been good about not whinin', but they've got to be needin' a rest," Micah said.

"We'd like to get home. We can rest there," Delia said firmly.

Tempest whimpered.

Fairlee heard it and shot her a mean look.

Tyrell dismounted and looped the reins of his horse around the hitching post in front of the hotel. The stores down the street were dark, only a saloon still showing light. He'd love to go there, have a drink, and talk to the men about the country ahead, but he was too blasted tired to do anything but fall into a bed and sleep. He'd slept little the night before after finding out that ferryman Harry was a thief and possibly worse, with a hungry eye out for Delia Lavalle. That they'd gotten out of the barn with only their supply of coffee gone missing was a miracle.

He went inside to find that there were

plenty of rooms available. He asked for four, and the clerk handed him four big skeleton keys on wooden tags with numbers written on them. "Two of the rooms are connected. Built them that way for families. The other two are across the hall and side by side. That a problem?"

"That's just fine. Are you still serving supper?"

"With whatever is left in the kitchen. The cook went home, but she made a big pot of soup today, and there's bread and cheese. I could rustle that much up," he said.

"If you'll set up a table for six, we'll be back as soon as we take our horses to the livery," Tyrell said.

"It will be ready. Baths? We got a bathing room on this floor. Got two tubs in it, and I can heat up some water," he said.

"No, we'll just have supper and go on to bed."

When they returned, a long, narrow table was laid out with bowls of steaming hot soup, two baskets of corn bread and one of crusty sourdough rolls, and two platters of sliced yellow cheese. Delia sat down, crumbled a two-inch square of corn bread into her soup, and began to eat. She couldn't remember anything ever tasting so good. She didn't realize Tyrell had sat down

137

beside her until she'd eaten several bites and her hand brushed his as she was reaching for a piece of cheese.

She didn't even try to convince herself that the tingle his skin against hers caused was due to fatigue or hunger. Not after that flush of plain old jealousy she experienced every time Micah mentioned the schoolmarm in Val Verde. She'd developed a reluctant attraction to the tall, brown-haired, green-eyed man with the slow southern drawl. He was well made, with no extra fat around his midsection. He was very, very handsome. She was a woman. She would have had to be graveyard dead or stone-cold blind not to be attracted to him. It meant nothing, though, and she'd forget him once she was home and back in her own element.

Tyrell ignored his own feelings and kept eating. Any man might be attracted to any one of the Lavalle sisters. They were all three lovely ladies. Tempest had the darkest eyes and had been named right. She could go from giggling like a schoolgirl to rage before a man could blink his eyes. Now that he thought about it, Fairlee was correctly named too — the most even-tempered of the sisters. Delia . . . Delia was the tallest, the most imposing, at — he stole a sidelong glance at her — maybe five and a half feet.

Her jet black hair was straight and flowed down past her waist. His hands itched to pull the pins out and let the silkiness of her tresses flow through his fingers. Her eyes were the lightest of all three sisters'. A blue that reminded him of creek water reflecting only the clearest of summer skies, so transparent that, if he leaned forward, he could see all the way to the bottom.

But he couldn't see the bottom of Delia's soul. The few times he'd looked right into her eyes, they'd been arguing, and she'd snapped a curtain shut. He wondered what it would be like to kiss those lips and watch the curtain fall, to see what awaited the man who earned the right to love her.

"We have four rooms tonight," he said. Maybe if he talked, he'd forget about Delia Lavalle and the effect she was having on him.

Delia turned and looked at him, and for a moment he thought he saw beyond the curtain, but before he could register anything more than a passing feeling of peace, she blinked.

"Why'd you do that?" she asked.

"They had extra rooms. I want one to myself. These two snorin' fellers can share one. You girls can divide up however you want. Your rooms have a connecting door.

The clerk said that they built a few that way for families," he said.

"Heaven," Tempest sighed.

"What're *you* talkin' about, Tempie?" Fairlee protested. "You've had your own bed every time we stopped in a town. No one can sleep with you — you kick and snore both," she said.

"Yes, but for once I won't have to look at your forlorn faces and feel guilty tonight. With two rooms, there's bound to be at least three beds, maybe four," Tempest told her.

"You never felt guilty about a thing in your life," Fairlee argued.

"How do you know?"

"Because you're the baby, and Momma doted on you," Fairlee said.

"Ladies, we don't air our dirty laundry in public," Delia chided.

"I do. We'll be gone from here tomorrow morning and probably won't ever come back. Who cares what anyone hears or repeats?" Tempest was on a tear. Her dark blue eyes were flashing, her jaw muscles constricting. She had a mad spell coming on, and nothing could stop it. When she got like that, it was best to just sit back and let her anger run out of steam.

Delia went back to her soup. Tempest was right in that they'd never come back through there again. Even if the Alamo stood and Santa Anna had already been buried, Robert Lavalle would never give his permission for his daughters to go back to Texas. The land was in the throes of birthing a new Republic, and it would take years before it was safe enough for Captain Lavalle to move his daughters from the haven he'd built for them in Louisiana.

So if the two younger sisters wanted to argue, fight, or even create a spectacle by rolling around on the floor scratching and snatching each other bald, she wasn't letting it interfere with her supper.

Fairlee cocked her head to one side and brushed back an errant strand of hair that had escaped the twist on top of her head.

"Delia?" she asked.

Tempest looked from one to the other. "Well?"

"You two started it. You finish it. I'm done with my meal. I'm taking one of these delicious rolls and a chunk of cheese up to the room for later. Don't come upstairs until you're both in a better mood. And remember this, if you get into a fight and tear up this dining room, you will pay for it out of your own money. I'm not paying for your fits," she said as she pushed back her chair.

The men started to stand, but she motioned for them to sit still. "Good night everyone. We'll be ready to ride out of here in the morning as usual."

She was halfway up the stairs when she heard an unfamiliar female voice and turned back to see a gorgeous woman with thick blond braids twisted around the top of her head like a crown. She wore a lovely dress along with a brilliant smile, and she stood beside Tyrell at the table.

"Mr. Fannin, what a lovely surprise to see you again. Did you catch that horrid man who killed your uncle?" the woman asked.

"In a manner of speaking. It's nice to see you again also. Are you still teaching school here in Val Verde?" Tyrell asked.

"Yes, I am. May I sit? Perhaps you'd introduce me to the ladies at your table. I already know your two cousins," she said.

Before Tyrell could get out a word, Delia had turned around on the stairs and headed back to the table.

"Hello. You must be the schoolteacher Micah told us about when we decided to stop here in Val Verde," she said as she marched across the room.

The lady's facial expression gave away her thoughts more than words could ever do. "And you would be . . . ?"

"My name is Delia, and I am Tyrell Fan-

142

nin's . . . 'wife.' I think you were about to sit in my chair. Perhaps you'd like to pull up another. That one is taken," Delia said.

She'd teach him to claim to be her husband in front of the Comanche. Payback could be very unpleasant, and he was about to get a taste of the way she'd felt when he'd sprung that on her in front of the chief. As Tempest had said, tomorrow they would leave and never return to this part of the world again, and Delia had money of her own if her sisters had to postpone their catfight for her to have one with the brazen flirt.

"I'm . . . M-Martha Anderson," the lady stammered.

Tempest and Fairlee were both grinning. What was Delia doing, claiming to be Tyrell's wife? Tyrell had told the Indians the same thing, but that was to save their lives. No one was in danger that evening — unless Tempest and Fairlee really got into a slap fest with each other.

Micah's mouth was hanging open, and Isaac silently watched the scene unfold. Tyrell had steam coming out of his ears, but there wasn't a thing he could say or do, or he'd look like a fool.

"Martha Anderson, these are my sisters, Tempest and Fairlee Lavalle." Delia pointed at each of them and slid back into her chair. "Our father is Captain Robert Lavalle, and he's among the defending forces at the Alamo."

Tyrell finally regained his composure and donned a wicked smile. "Yep. It was love at first sight, Miss Anderson. I thought Delia here was one of God's angels," he said as he threw his arm over the back of her chair.

The impetuousness of her actions immediately began to take its toll on Delia. Tyrell's touch was like fire through the fabric of her shirt. Still, she vowed she wouldn't let him or Martha Anderson get ahead of her.

"And I thought he was an outlaw," Delia said sweetly.

"We shall leave you all to visit a while with Miss Anderson. Delia and I are retiring for the night." Tyrell stood up and held out a hand to Delia.

Although trembling at his charade and her own audacity, she placed her small hand in his. "Good night. It was very nice to meet you, Miss Anderson," she managed to say.

Martha's face turned as red as the setting sun. "It was nice to see you again, Mr. Fannin, and to meet you, Mrs. Fannin. I wish you a safe journey."

Tyrell kept his hand on Delia's back all

the way up the stairs, and his touch felt like a brand. When they reached the rooms, he pulled a key from his pocket. "Shall I carry you over the threshold? We haven't had a proper honeymoon, but tonight I have a room that's separate from the others."

Delia propped her hands on her hips. "You could say thank you instead of making such an indecent proposal."

"Thank you for what, *Mrs. Fannin?*"

"For saving your sorry hide. That woman would have kept you at the table for at least an hour or more. And there was a large party of people and other ladies present, so she could claim it was a group discussion and she was not enlisting the attention of a single man, risking losing her dignity or her job. But it was evident she'd have flirted all evening, and you're already grouchy, so, 'Thank you, Delia Lavalle, for saving me so I can get a good night's sleep,' " she said without stopping for a breath.

Mrs. Fannin indeed! Hell had not frozen over yet, and it would have to before anyone, especially this man, could use that title on her!

"I will get even, Delia," he smiled.

"No, now we *are* even. You called me your wife in front of that Comanche chief and made me want to chew nails. I just got even.

It's over," she said.

"I don't think so, Mrs. Fannin. If you won't let me carry you over the threshold, then this will have to do," he said.

"What are you talking about?" She looked up in time to see his face nearing hers at an alarming rate and to feel his arms drawing her close to his chest. And then his lips covered hers.

It was not at all like the few stolen kisses she'd experienced before. That night in Val Verde, Texas, Delia found out what a kiss was all about and how it could affect a woman's ability to think.

Everything stopped except the racing of her heart and the churning in her stomach. Time stood still. She was sure the earth stopped moving altogether. There was no time for analyzing anything. She leaned in for more, never wanting the burst of emotions to cease.

Then it ended, and everything started up again at a dizzying speed.

"Why — why did you do that?" she gasped.

"Because you are my 'wife,' and that's the way a husband kisses a wife," he said.

"Good night, Tyrell." She hid her trembling hands and marched across the hallway to her room.

Her mind kept screaming in a deafening voice the whole time she fumbled with the key. *If that's the way a husband kisses a wife, then maybe I dang sure do want a husband. Maybe I'll go hunt for an eligible bachelor as soon as I get home. God Almighty, what have I been missing?*

CHAPTER NINE

Delia was so stunned from Tyrell's kiss that she sank down in a rocking chair hard enough to set it rocking. She touched her burning lips. Did husbands really kiss wives like that? No wonder her mother had stayed with her father all those years despite his frequent expeditions, if she got that kind of feeling when he came home.

She was so shocked that when the door opened, she half expected to see Tyrell bursting in to kiss her again. Disappointment set in when only Tempest and Fairlee rushed into the room.

Tempest plopped down on the side of a bed and stared at Delia. "You look like you're about to faint. I can't believe you did that, but it's nothing to go all white over. It wasn't like you, Delia. It was more like what I would have done in a fit of anger."

Fairlee slapped Delia on the knee. "The look on Tyrell's face was priceless. He was so mad, I swear I saw steam coming out of his nose like a rangy old bull when it sees red. What did he say when he walked you up the stairs? Is he going to leave us to our own devices to get home? I probably would if I was in his shoes, but it would be worth it. Micah and Isaac are still in shock, and that schoolmarm made excuses in a hurry and rushed out the front door. It was so funny, I forgot I was mad at Tempie."

"We're waiting," Tempest said to Delia.

Delia found her voice, but it came out high and squeaky. "I don't have any idea why I claimed to be Mrs. Fannin, except that that woman made me mad. Waltzing into the dining room in her pretty dress and lacy shawl with her light hair fixed just so. It's been so long since I got to dress up and have my hair all pretty that it made me mad."

"What'd Tyrell say?" Fairlee asked again.

"He asked me if I wanted him to carry me over the threshold," Delia confessed, red-faced. That was enough. She would never admit to the kiss even if she had to tell an out-and-out lie and go to hell for it.

Tempest held her breath. "Was that a proposal?"

Tyrell Fannin wouldn't be the man *she* chose for Delia, but if he proposed and

149

Delia accepted, then she'd only have to get Fairlee married off when they got back home. And then it would be her turn, and that was the goal she had in mind.

Delia swore. "Jesus, Mary, and Joseph!"

"Momma would wash out your mouth for that! Besides, you were a Catholic nun for a while, and they don't use those names as swear words," Tempest said.

"Well, did Tyrell ask you to marry him?" Fairlee demanded.

"He did not!" Delia said.

"Well, rats," Tempest said.

Delia went to the washstand to begin her nightly ritual. It was an excellent excuse to hide her face from her sisters. Lord, if they ever figured out that she'd been kissed, they'd have her marching down the aisle at the church for sure when they got home.

"Why do you want me to get married to an almost stranger?" she asked Tempest as she washed her face.

"Tyrell Fannin isn't a stranger. He was two weeks ago when we left San Antonio, but he's not now," Fairlee pointed out.

Delia changed tack. "So if the men aren't strangers, why don't you bat your eyelashes at Micah?"

Fairlee huffed. "That's disgusting. Neither he nor Isaac Burnet appeal to me."

"How about you, Tempie?" Delia asked.

"I'd rather be courted by one of the Baker twins, and you know how I feel about them," she said.

"You were 'wives' to the Burnets at the same time I was to Tyrell Fannin when we were in the Comanche village. So what if I wanted to marry *you* off to *them?*"

"Tyrell looks at you all . . . different. As if he might like you but doesn't know what to do about it," Fairlee said.

Delia combed out her hair. "Y'all ever think that he might already be married or have a woman waiting to marry him? For that matter, maybe Isaac and Micah do too. Micah is the youngest one of the three, and he's twenty-two — well past the time when he could have taken a wife."

That stopped her younger sisters for a while.

"Well, if Tyrell's got a wife or a fiancée at home, I'm glad I'm not that woman, because then he's got a wandering eye, Delia Lavalle, and it's settled on you," Tempest said. "And now I'm going to get ready for bed. At the rate we're going, we should be home at Oak View in another two weeks."

"I should hope so." Delia stripped down to her undergarments and turned back the quilt covering the bed. The sheets were crisp and smelled like sunshine and outdoors. She was suddenly homesick and thought of her aunt and uncle and of the Lavalle girls' nanny. Rosy would be as tickled to see them as Rachel and Jonathan. She hadn't wanted them to go off on a lark to the fort in Texas, and she'd fuss and fume about being right, but it would be so good to be back home to listen to her carrying on.

Fairlee and Tempest left the door open between the two rooms, and she could hear them whispering as they wriggled into their beds. At least there hadn't been a fight that would require payment or jail time before they could leave the next morning; Fairlee and Tempie were now giggling together. Delia shut her eyes and truly wished the next two weeks were already past.

Then her eyelids flew open. "Two weeks," she mumbled with a groan, then bit her lip to keep from making another noise.

Two whole weeks, and she'd have to face Tyrell Fannin every single day. After a steamy kiss that should only be shared by a married couple, how in the devil was she supposed to face him the next morning? Did he think she was a loose woman for letting him kiss her like that? But she hadn't let him, not really; she simply hadn't slapped his face or pushed him away.

She'd liked the kiss! By golly, she had, and if she had her way, she'd get out of bed and go try out another one. That thought brought on another flush that lit up her face as if a lamp had been turned on. She was almighty glad her sisters were in the other room, or there'd be dozens of questions.

"Nothing can be done about it now. What's done is done," she mumbled, and she forced herself to go to sleep.

She awoke early as usual, dressed quietly, and was having breakfast of eggs and biscuits with a side order of fried potatoes and beefsteak when Tyrell pulled out the chair across the table from her.

"Good morning," he said formally.

Had she dreamed the kiss?

"Good morning," she said.

He poured himself a cup of coffee and told the man waiting tables that he would have the same thing the lady was having.

"Sleep well?" he asked.

"Very well, thank you. The room was quite nice. Yours?"

"Much better than the barn and worryin' about that ferryman," Tyrell said.

"Well, are we going to talk about what happened or ignore it?" She looked right at him.

He raised one eyebrow. "What? That you

153

got even with me?"

"You know exactly what I mean," she said.

He let the eyebrow fall to match the other one. "How old are you? I know that's an inappropriate thing to ask a lady — my mother did teach me manners before she died with the cholera — but I'd like an answer. You can even cheat a year on either end if you'd like."

"I'm twenty-one, and that's the truth. No cheating."

"I'm twenty-eight. We're adults. We shared a kiss. That doesn't mean we have to marry. It doesn't mean that you were anything other than honorable. It was a kiss. It was . . . nice. We were both tired and playing roles you cast us in with your remark about being my wife. It's over now. Forget about it," he said, wishing he could.

The food arrived, and he picked up his fork.

What Tyrell had said sounded reasonable, but suddenly Delia wanted to slap him cross-eyed. It was over — that much was true. It was a kiss; yes, sir, it definitely was that. And it might have been brought on by her throwing them into unfamiliar territory with her remark. But it was much more than *nice;* it had come close to giving Delia the vapors. And she'd never had a fainting spell in her life.

"So?" he asked.

"Like you said, I shall forget it ever happened. It wasn't that great anyway. I can understand why you aren't married, if that's the best you can do," she said as if she were discussing whether it might rain or not.

Tyrell almost spewed coffee across the table before he got control of himself and swallowed the mouthful of hot liquid. He'd thought he buckled her knees with that kiss, and she'd about sent *him* down on one knee to propose right there in the hotel hallway. *Not that great?* How many men had she kissed anyway, and what more did she want?

"Here come Tempie and Fairlee. If your cousins can haul their sleepy bodies out of bed, we could get an early start this morning. I'd rather we didn't discuss this again, Mr. Fannin," she said firmly.

"I can't see any reason we should," he said coldly.

"Good. Will we be camping this evening, or is there a settlement nearby where we will end up?" She had regained a semblance of composure by the time her sisters were seated.

"I've talked to the man who owns this place. Other than a few scattered families trying to fend off the Indians, there's nothing ahead for at least a week. We could go due north and hit a small settlement town tonight, then it would be a couple of days on the trail until we find another, but that route would add another week to the trip. You decide," Tyrell said.

"Take us by the shortest route you can," Tempest said without hesitation. "I can sleep sitting up against a tree after a hard day's ride just as easily as I can in a bed."

Delia turned to her middle sister. "Fairlee?"

"I want to go home. Let's just get there," she said.

"You heard them. We'll take the shortest route," Delia said. At least there would be no bedroom doors or hallways. The vastness of sky and earth wasn't nearly as conducive to kisses as dimly lit hotel hallways.

CHAPTER TEN

Dark clouds were rolling in from the south-west, and small sparks of lightning were visible when they rode their horses across a narrow bend in the Trinity at dusk. A storm was approaching, and no place on the either side of the river offered shelter. But oak trees covered most of the area, and there was dry wood, so Isaac and Tyrell got busy making a fire while Micah unsaddled the horses and tethered them to feed on spring grasses. If they hurried, they might get a meal together before the storm hit; if not, they'd be wet *and* hungry.

Delia had purchased enough ham for that evening and perhaps the next day's lunch before they left the inn. The lady had also sold her a new jar of bacon renderings, so she had grease for the next week. If they could shoot a deer or a wild turkey or even a couple of rabbits, it would help. She missed the fare at their plantation, Oak

View. Their cook, a big round lady who bossed the kitchen help like a brigadier general, could make anything. Their evening meal always had at least half a dozen vegetables, two choices of meat, and numerous desserts. Fanny had been with the Lavalle family since before they had a plantation in Louisiana, way back when the Lavalle brothers, Robert and Jonathan, were born. The nanny, Rosy, was the only other servant who'd been around longer. The three Lavalle girls made three generations of Lavalles that she'd made toe the line.

"What are you thinking about?" Tyrell asked.

He was close enough that she felt his breath on her neck. So much for thinking that a hotel hallway was the only place for intimacy. Tingles danced up and down her spine, and she shivered.

She kept slicing ham and frying each piece in the hot grease. "I was thinking about Fanny."

"Who?"

"Our cook. I was thinking about what they might be having for supper tonight at the plantation," she said.

"You own a plantation?" he asked.

She left the ham long enough to stir up bread dough in the pot she used for beans and stews. "My uncle and my father own the plantation. My father has always been a military man, so he comes and goes. Uncle Jonathan was close to the soil his entire life, so he takes care of the property. He has two sons, both older than us three girls, and they'll inherit the property eventually. They're both married and live on the plantation."

"What do you grow?"

"Cotton mostly," she said.

Tyrell would ask anything to keep Delia talking. She had a husky tone that offset the southern sweetness. He could have spent the whole night right there listening to her recite the alphabet or read the Bible. "You don't mind watching men inherit your home?"

She forked the last piece of ham from the grease and started dropping biscuits in. "It's the way we live these days. When it changes, we'll all change with it."

She looked up at the darkening sky and changed the subject. "What happens when it starts to rain?"

"We get wet," he said.

She pointed at the lazy stream so close that the horses could drink from their tether ropes. "That river going to swell?"

Tempest and Fairlee came back from a

trip to the bushes and stood beside Delia. "What happens if the river does swell?" Tempest asked.

Tyrell shrugged. "We gather up our gear and move out, or we get washed away."

"Maybe the storm will circle around us," Fairlee said hopefully.

She didn't get her wish. They made sandwiches from ham and chunks of hoecake, ate hurriedly, and unrolled their blankets. Tyrell took the first watch and woke them all two hours later.

"Must be raining up north. River is rising, and thunder is rumbling. We've got to move out before the water gets any higher."

Delia wanted to whine. She really did. Just a little. But it would do absolutely no good. She couldn't control the weather any more than she could control her dreams about Tyrell Fannin and that kiss that had sent her into shock. She was on her feet, bent over and rolling up her sleeping roll, when a clap of thunder jarred her fully awake. One look at the river told her Tyrell was telling the truth. The sweet little stream they'd crossed earlier was already rolling furiously, throwing debris to both sides. There must have been a devil of a lot of rain upstream. Maybe they could stay far enough ahead of the storm to at least remain dry.

They'd ridden about two miles when they saw a tornado in the distance, twisting and turning like a black funnel, touching the earth and sweeping back up, dancing toward them. That's when they spotted a farmhouse chimney standing like a lighthouse, beckoning the tornado to come fight with it.

Tempest shouted over the sound of the wind as it howled through the trees. "I wonder if those folks have a root cellar under their house."

Tyrell broke away from the rest and rode ahead at a faster speed. They watched as he bailed off the horse and searched for a door that could lead to a cellar of any kind. He shook his head and jumped back on the horse. He'd ridden no more than a hundred feet when he drew up the reins and motioned at them.

The wooden door was charred where the barn had burned and the hinges sounded like the squawk of a buzzard when Tyrell threw it open. He tied his horse to the nearest tree and hoped for the best. He'd seen a few of those funnel clouds, and they could pick up a horse or a cow and leave the animal in the branches of a tree or worse. If it picked up their horses, it could easily toss them away like rubbish into the river, and they'd never find the beasts.

161

He went ahead of the rest, brushing away spiderwebs and kicking at a scurrying mouse. The cellar had been shored up very well with timbers and had a tunnel in one side. Probably an escape hatch in case of an Indian raid. Shelves lined the walls. At one time a prairie wife had likely had hopes of filling them with canned goods from her garden. A basket of potatoes sat in a corner with green sprouts sticking out. The place smelled like smoke.

"Mother Nature is a fickle old girl," Delia said as she hurried her sisters down the cellar steps. Isaac and Micah pushed in behind them, and the first drops of rain pelted Tyrell's head as he pulled the door down. They were in total darkness for a few minutes before Isaac got a small fire built off to one side of the cellar.

"Close quarters. It could get . . . ." Isaac stopped when everything went silent as a tomb.

Then the roaring wind hit, and Delia covered her ears.

Tempest almost cried.

Fairlee shut her eyes and promised she'd never wear another nun's habit if they wouldn't be sucked up and thrown into the raging river.

It lasted ten minutes, and suddenly the

silence was as deafening as the roaring noise. Heavy breathing and the soft crackle of the fire sounded like gun shots and ferocious wind combined.

Delia looked at Tyrell. "Is it over?"

He nodded.

"I hope the horses are still alive," Isaac said.

Tyrell pushed against the door, but it wouldn't open. Isaac came to help. Still nothing. Micah lent his shoulder to the effort, but the door wouldn't budge. It must have been covered with debris. They could see shadows between the charred boards, but the door wasn't giving an inch.

Delia gasped. They were literally buried alive. After all they'd survived and been through, it didn't seem fair.

"The tunnel," Tyrell said.

Everyone looked at him as if he'd grown an extra nose.

He kicked dirt over the fire and extinguished the flames. "It's got to be open because the smoke is traveling that way. We'll have to put out the fire and feel our way along or else the smoke will kill us."

"It's right there. See it?" Micah said.

"We'll give it a few minutes, then I'll crawl through and see if there's an escape hatch on the other end. If so, I'll see what can be done about getting that door open," Tyrell said.

Delia's palms went clammy as the last red embers of the fire died. "What if . . ."

Tyrell gave the smoke time to clear out of the tunnel. "It's the only way. The door won't budge, and we've got to get out of here."

He stuck his head into the hole and felt ahead of him. A few spiderwebs, but timbers shored up the tunnel. He crawled inside. "I'll yell every few feet to let you know how I'm doing."

Delia held her breath until she felt faint, then let it out in a loud whoosh. Tempest patted her leg, and Fairlee reached across the dark space and grasped her hand.

"It's safe so far, but I can't see light at the end yet," Tyrell called.

A few minutes later, they heard him again, this time not as loudly. "Still going. No light yet."

Thick tension filled the root cellar as Tyrell's voice became fainter and fainter. Finally they could hear him no more, and Delia's heart beat so fast and hard, she feared it would jump out of her chest and race down the tunnel after him. It was merely about survival, she told herself. It had nothing to do with that kiss. If Tyrell couldn't get through the hole to the outside, they'd die in a root cellar. Her father and her aunt and uncle would never know what became of them.

Poor, poor Father. When he came back to Louisiana for a visit, expecting to see his grown girls come running out of the house to greet him, there would be only the news that Uncle Jonathan thought they were with him in San Antonio all those months.

Time had no meaning in the darkness of the cellar. Had they waited an hour, or had it only been a few minutes? Was it two hours or three that had sped by in their fear, or merely fifteen minutes that had stuck somewhere in eternity? No one spoke for fear that Tyrell's voice would float through the tunnel and they wouldn't hear.

"Well, I'll be damned," he said, loud and clear.

Delia stuck out her hand to see if he was right in front of her.

"Where are you?" she called.

"That damn chimney fell over," Tyrell said from the other side of the cellar door.

Delia didn't even care that he was swearing or that he was on the outside and she wasn't.

"What do we do?" Isaac asked.

"You and Micah come on out through the

tunnel. It ends up south of here in a grove of oak trees. It's safe. I left the door on the other end open."

Isaac and Micah were already in the tunnel by the time he finished, taking turns yelling back every few feet, just as Tyrell had done.

"Can't we come out that way too?" Delia asked.

"We'll get you out. It's stopped raining now, and the stars are shining. Everything is wet, so we'll ride farther before we make camp again," Tyrell said.

"The horses? Are they there?" Delia asked.

"I'm going to check on them. Stay put, and don't crawl into that tunnel. Promise me," Tyrell said.

Delia hesitated.

"She promises. See about our horses," Tempest said.

"Why did you do that?" Delia asked the space where Tempest's voice had come from.

"Because I don't want to walk the rest of the way to Louisiana, and I want to know if the horses are all right. If you didn't promise, he would stay right there and keep talking so he'd know we weren't in the tunnel. Evidently it isn't as safe as he says," Tempest told her.

Goose bumps popped up on Delia's arms and neck, and she listened carefully for the Burnet brothers' voices.

"We're out and right here," Isaac said.

Delia's scalp stopped crawling when she heard them.

"Let's get started," Isaac said.

"What do you have to do?" Delia asked.

"Take it apart. The mortar is old. I can't figure how that storm put it here without it breaking all apart," Isaac said.

"It won't work that way," Micah said.

Delia gasped.

"Don't do that," Tempest hissed. "It scares me worse than that chimney on the door."

Delia forced herself to inhale and exhale evenly.

"Use a tree limb," Tyrell said. "I'll help you find one. Put it under the top part, and we'll all put our weight on it. Maybe the thing will roll off."

"Horses?" Tempest yelled.

"Six of them. No pack mule. What's left of the pack is blown up against a tree. We'll salvage what we can. At least the horses are alive and unharmed."

Tempest squealed.

"Is she all right?" Tyrell asked.

Delia raised her voice to be heard. "She's fine. Just excited about the horses."

"Okay, now push down with all you've got," Micah said.

A great rumble, not unlike thunder, sounded as the chimney rolled free of the cellar door. In the next moment Tyrell had it open and his hand out to help the sisters. "Step easy, over the top of the rocks. The mortar broke when it rolled, but it's off the door now."

"Oh, my!" Delia looked at the countryside. Trees were down all around them, but the small grove where they'd tied their horses was untouched. The mule was gone, as Tyrell had said. Micah whistled shrilly, but the animal didn't come wandering out of the woods.

"Luck kissed us today," Tyrell said.

At the mention of a kiss, Delia blushed. She was glad it was still dark enough that no one could see her cheeks. Or if they did, maybe they'd think it was due to the fact that she'd been scared out of her wits.

"So do we ride on or sleep in the cellar?" Tyrell asked.

"I vote to ride, but it should be your call, since you're the one who's had no sleep," Micah said.

Tyrell brushed back his hair and settled his hat onto his head. "I can sleep later. We'll stop early this afternoon and rest. You all have only had two more hours than I have."

"What time is it?" Delia asked.

He checked his watch. "Three-fifteen. Couple of hours until sunup."

"The horses are saddled. We might as well go on," she said.

"I'll throw what's left of the pack on behind me. We can divide up the remains when we stop," Micah offered.

Tyrell nodded as he removed a compass from his pocket and studied it. North by northeast was what they'd been traveling. He'd keep it that way. He pointed in the direction they'd go and mounted his horse. The saddle was wet, but at least it wasn't freezing cold, and when the sun came up, it would soon dry out.

They followed the rain, seeing the clouds ahead of them, for most of the morning before the storm finally moved far enough away that they couldn't see it anymore. By noon they were all ready for a break and found the shell of an abandoned barn. The roof had holes the size of dinner plates peppered through it. Weathered planks covered the outer walls that listed to the south, but there was a well to one side that had good water and the remnants of hay left in the loft for the horses.

"I'm starving," Isaac said as they slid off their mounts.

"If you'll take care of the animals, I'll be glad to get a fire going and make food," Delia said.

Micah untied the pack and laid it out on the ground. The bacon grease was there. Flour and soda too, but the top half of the flour was wet. The sugar was gone. No meat except for a parcel of jerky. One skillet but no lid and no bean pot.

"We've each got a tin plate and cup in our saddlebags, right?" Delia had worked with less on the trail but not by much.

"I found some coffee!" Micah shouted.

"That's a blessing." Delia smiled. "All we'll have is jerky and hoecakes, but that will feed us enough that we can sleep a little while. Too bad I didn't pick up a few of those sprouting potatoes."

Tempest yawned. "Anything to fill me up, and then I'm sleeping forever."

Isaac and Micah shored up the stables and put the horses inside. Using a rope and bucket they found in the loft, they drew enough water to satisfy the animals. They pulled up one final bucketful for drinking with dinner.

Fairlee climbed the ladder and took stock of the loft. Their bedrolls were wet, but they could hang them on the horse stalls to dry and sleep on the hay. She poked around in it with the butt of her gun, making sure there were no hidden snakes or rats.

Delia fried bread, turning it carefully when the bottom was crispy brown. She divided it six ways when it was done and put another skillet on to cook while they ate the first biscuits.

Micah yawned. "I'm glad we had enough left to make bread."

"Me too," Tempest agreed.

That was the extent of the conversation. One by one, they finished eating and climbed the ladder to the loft, where each one claimed a section of hay-covered floor. Delia put out the fire and cleaned her one remaining pan. She arranged what supplies they had left on a shelf in what had been the tack room. Then she crawled up the ladder. Lifting one foot in front of the other took up every ounce of the remainder of her energy.

Tempest and Fairlee were curled up in little knots on the west side of the loft. Isaac and Micah were as far to the east as they could get, stretched out on their backs, so tired they weren't even snoring. Tyrell was sitting next to the window, looking out over the countryside.

She sat down beside him. "You should be asleep."

"I will be in a minute. I just wanted to be sure there were no Harry-the-ferryman-type men lurking in the shadows of this old barn," he said.

"We could all sleep for a while. It's broad daylight. Surely we're safe for now," Delia said.

"Go on and rest. I'll sleep soon," he said.

She continued to sit there until her head bobbled against her chest. When she started to topple over to one side, he caught her and gently laid her back in the hay right beside him.

What would it be like to wake up beside this magnificent woman every morning until they were so old that one of them was called on to eternity? She was a woman any man would be proud to ride the river with, who'd stand beside her husband instead of hiding behind his back. A jolt of jealousy streaked through him as he thought about another man kissing Delia. He had no right to be jealous — he could never offer her a lifestyle comparable to what she had back in Louisiana — but he was. He fell back and stared out over Texas, wishing he'd met Delia Lavalle under different circumstances.

They slept through supper, through the

172

night, and didn't awaken until an hour before daybreak the next day. Delia opened her eyes and pushed away Fairlee's hand. But it wasn't Fairlee's arm pinning her down. And it wasn't Fairlee's breath on her neck. She'd slept in Tyrell's arms all night! She sat up with a start and moved to one side.

Tyrell opened his eyes lazily and realized what had happened. He'd had no intentions of sleeping beside Delia. He'd planned to move when he got drowsy.

"So, shall I make an honest woman out of you?" he teased.

"Shh! They'll wake up and hear you," she scolded.

"Too late. We slept together. What's that going to do to your chances of finding a decent husband?" he whispered as he sat up.

"I'm going to ignore you and what happened. I'm going down the ladder to start some food. It'll just be bread again, but maybe we can find a farm sometime today, and the lady will sell us a few supplies," she said.

"Delia, we didn't sin. We just fell asleep," he said seriously.

She was moving down the ladder and didn't reply.

His arms ached to hold her a while longer, to sink his face into her black hair. She fit so well in his arms, and he'd slept better than he had since they started the trip, back when he and his cousins were outlaws and the Lavalle sisters were angels.

CHAPTER ELEVEN

Delia rode through Cherokee country beside Tyrell, with Isaac and Fairlee riding behind them and Micah and Tempest bringing up the rear. It had been more than two weeks since they'd left the Alamo, and they'd had very little information. Had the battle gone to the Mexicans, or were the Texans still holding them off? Was Father all right? Was he still alive? Delia went to sleep each night with unanswered questions and awoke every morning with the same questions on her mind. For the most part she didn't voice them aloud to keep from upsetting her sisters.

That morning she waited until the others had lagged behind and asked Tyrell, "Do you think the battle is over? Did the Alamo stand?"

Tyrell was watching every movement in the landscape, hoping they didn't encounter another situation like they'd had with the

Comanche. He remembered the caves that one tribe of Cherokee lived in and kept an eye peeled to the north for them. With a little luck the braves would keep to their caves and ignore the six people riding through their country. It was the first time Tyrell was glad the women did not ride sidesaddle and that they wore trousers. From a distance they could be mistaken for men.

That thought brought him around to a vision of Delia out of trousers and in a dress, her long black hair flowing down her back. Her question, too, had brought him up short.

"You want the truth or a sweet lie?" he asked seriously.

"The truth."

"I don't think those soldiers had a chance with that many of Santa Anna's men surrounding them. I don't have a doubt in my mind that every one of them went down fighting and took a bunch of that Mexican army out with them, but I figure the Alamo fell to the Mexicans."

"I pray that my father got out alive. I wouldn't even care if he escaped and ran like a coward and is hiding somewhere."

"Maybe in a nun's habit?" he asked.

"Don't tease. I'm very serious about this.

I have a feeling that he's dead, but I can't talk to my sisters about it. They might get hysterical," she whispered.

"Don't bury him or his memory without solid evidence. Those old soldiers are wily and tough. We three offered to fight with them if the sheriff would let us out of jail, but he said they'd win by their wits, and three more men wouldn't make enough difference for us to stay," Tyrell said.

Delia shivered. Likely Tyrell, too, would be dead if he had stayed and fought with the Texans. To lose her father would be devastating; to lose both him and Tyrell — she refused to even think about that.

She quickly changed the subject. "Why are we riding so slowly?"

"We're in Cherokee country now. No doubt they've seen us, but if we go riding hell-bent through here, they'll give chase. They're like the Comanche in that they respect honesty and fearlessness. They can smell fear a hundred miles away. Speed would make us look afraid. Let them watch us ride slowly as if we're confident, and perhaps they'll let us pass through their land without incident."

"After that business with the Comanche, I *am* afraid," she said.

"You? I thought you could reform Lucifer

and turn hell into an iceberg." Tyrell chuckled.

"I might. But these days I'm not nearly as afraid of the devil as I am of those Indians."

"Don't ever let them know it. If they come riding up, whooping and hollerin', or if they just appear suddenly beside you, don't let on that you're afraid."

"Will we still be on their land tonight when we stop?" she asked.

"We'll be on their land until we cross into Louisiana. You got any idea how far into Louisiana your place is?"

"Twenty-five miles over the border is Bennett's Bluff. It's another ten to our plantation. Oak View lies between the Red Chute River and the Bayou Dorcheat — a little closer to the bayou, actually," she said. "How much farther is it to your home?"

"At least another week, but there'll be hotels and towns along the way, so the traveling will be easier," he said.

And you won't have three Lavalle women to worry about, she thought.

Wildflowers carpeted the earth in brilliant shades of blue, red, and yellow. Delia raised her eyes, and the bright purple redbuds and white dogwoods vied for her attention. In between the flowers and trees were low-lying blackberry brambles with their tiny white blossoms and wild plum thickets covered with blooms. She spotted two rabbits sitting beside a log and started for her gun when Tyrell reached out and covered her hand with his.

"No shooting today," he said. "Besides, you traded your gun for Hannah Marie, remember?"

She nodded and pulled a knife from the other side of her saddle. He did the same. They threw at the same moment, and neither missed the target. Tyrell retrieved the rabbits and tied them to his saddle horn before taking Delia's knife, wiping it clean, and handing it back to her.

She replaced it, and they kept riding. At least that night they'd have meat to go with their fried bread.

Without stopping for a rest, they chewed on jerky for dinner and had water from their canteens. The afternoon wore on in tension and silence. Every minute lasted an hour, and each hour felt just short of eternity. By the time the sun had passed its peak and was settling toward the west, Delia was as jumpy as a new bride. They'd ridden out of a wooded area when the wind whipped the smell of smoke around them.

In the next instant they spotted another burned-out farm ahead. They rode toward it cautiously, looking for raiders.

They were met by the bawling of a cow and a calf so newly born that it was still wet. The pigpen was nothing more than churned-up dirt. A few stray chickens scratched at the ground behind the house.

"The raiding party hasn't been gone long," Tyrell said.

"Does that mean we dismount or keep riding?" Delia asked.

"Want a chicken to go with the rabbits for supper?"

Delia nodded. "But I'd rather be away from here if there's a chance the raiders will come back."

"They won't be coming back anytime soon. They've already taken what they wanted. It's probably the safest place. Me and the boys will scout around and see which way they went. We don't want to follow them." He slid off his horse, then caught two chickens and wrung their necks. He handed them to Delia, who was still in the saddle. She tied them to her saddle horn.

Tempest cocked her head to one side and held up a hand. "Listen."

Delia's pulse raced as she strained her ears, but the only thing she heard was the rapid pounding of her own heart. "Are they coming back?" she asked.

"I don't hear a thing," Micah said.

"It's a kitten — out in the barn," Fairlee said. "I bet it's stuck up in the loft."

Tempest turned her horse and rode toward the remnants of the smoldering barn.

"Tempie, come back. You can't go in there. You could get hurt," Delia said.

Tempest pulled the reins back on the horse and held up a hand. "It's not a cat," she said.

She rode a few more feet, then dismounted and led her horse, listening intently the whole way. The rest of the party followed a few feet behind her.

She circled the barn. Nothing could have lived through the fire. The dry hay had provided fodder to burn the structure even faster than the house. Cats, rats, or humans wouldn't have survived. No, the sound wasn't coming from the barn. The noise that kept coming and going from somewhere nearby was weeping, and it sounded more like a child than a kitten. She shielded her eyes with the one hand and scanned the land as far as she could see.

Nothing.

Bringing her gaze closer, she saw a lump of garments not fifty feet behind the barn. She eased up to it. Tyrell was now on one side of her and Isaac on the other. Tyrell had a gun in his hand. Isaac held a knife.

The lump didn't move, but she could see calico and a bonnet. It was a woman, and she was injured! Tempest started running and fell down on her knees when she reached the woman. Her stomach turned, and she covered her mouth. The woman was dead, a bullethole in her back. Her bonnet was off to one side, and her gold wedding ring glittered in the sunlight. No amount of blinking or looking away erased the heartbreaking sight burned into Tempest's mind.

Well, she'd see to it that the woman had a proper burial, even if it meant riding all night to make up the lost time. Then she heard the soft mewling again. Was the woman somehow still alive and whimpering? When she bent over to check the woman's neck for a pulse, she saw where the noise had come from. The woman had literally wrapped herself around her baby when she fell. Tempest reached down and gently picked up the child wrapped tightly in a flannel blanket, with only its face showing. It looked up at her with big round eyes and whimpered.

"My God, it's a baby!" Tyrell said.

"And it's alive. But not its mother. We have to bury her before we go on," Fairlee said, echoing her sister's thought.

"How will we keep a baby alive?" Tyrell wondered aloud.

"With that cow over there," Fairlee said.

"Bringing a cow will slow us down for miles every day," he pointed out.

Delia took charge. "We will milk the cow and carry as much as we can with us. Then we'll find a farmhouse or someplace to buy more milk every day. We can't take the cow, and we can't leave this child to die."

Micah and Isaac began searching for a shovel or something to dig a grave with but had no luck. The barn was still too hot to get inside. Even the chicken coop had been burned.

Delia unsheathed her knife and said, "Use this to dig in the corral. The dirt will be softer there. Then put the woman in and cover her with rocks. That's the best we can do. I'll milk the cow. Fairlee, take care of the child. Tempie, you and Isaac stand guard while Tyrell and Micah bury the lady."

No one argued with her.

Delia poured the water from her canteen. She talked low and sweet to the cow as she led her to a tree stump and sat down.

"I'm not taking so much that your baby won't get its fill, just enough to keep that tiny child from starving. I bet you could tell us exactly what happened here and who did it. I wish you could talk," she whispered. If anyone thought she was crazy for talking to a cow, then so be it.

She'd been taught to milk, but she'd never liked the job. She carefully filled the canteen, squirting almost as much over the sides as she got inside. She'd have to figure out a way to get the milk into the child without a nipple. Maybe they'd pass a settlement that had a general store in the next few days, and she could purchase a real nursing bottle. Even better would be a farmhouse with a mother who'd sell them one.

What would they do with the baby when they got home? Aunt Rachel would take it in — no doubt about that. She had a heart and soul as big as her bosom, and that was enormous.

Tempest and Isaac kept a watchful eye on the area, but every so often she glanced back at her sister. She had been so thankful when Hannah's mother had appeared in the hotel they'd stopped at. Now Delia had a helpless little baby, and its mother was lying in a shallow grave, with Tyrell and Micah covering her with rocks. Delia would take charge of the baby and never marry.

Despite her natural sympathy for the babe

and its mother, Tempest groaned. She'd never find a husband at this rate. If Delia didn't marry, then Fairlee wouldn't feel right about wedding, and that would leave Tempest, who wanted a husband, out in the cold.

When Delia's canteen was filled with milk and the last rock piled on the grave, the group soberly mounted up to ride again.

"Let me carry the baby. All I did was stand guard, so I'll take the first shift," Tempest offered.

Fairlee handed it to her, and she cradled it against her chest with one hand and held the reins with the other. It must have nursed or fed recently, because it didn't fuss or chew on its little fingers. It simply slept in her arms most of the afternoon.

At dusk Tyrell found a place under a canopy of oak trees for them to camp. The trees offered a little protection in case of attack, and there was an old circle of rocks already there, where another passerby had made camp.

Delia fried the chicken and rabbit and made biscuits.

Isaac and Micah scouted the area for signs of Indians.

Tyrell tethered the horses and stood guard.

"It's a girl," Tempest announced. She'd removed the baby's nappy, washed it in a little water from her canteen, and hung it on a tree limb to dry. She tore a blanket into pieces for new nappies and wrapped the baby in her coat. She'd begun to whimper, so she slowly spoon-fed her milk until she slept again.

"I wonder where the man of the house was," Tyrell mused aloud.

"Probably in the barn, dead. They all might have hidden there, and the woman ran out to save her baby when the flames got too hot," Delia said somberly.

"I hope he wasn't foolish enough to leave his woman and child there unprotected. Can you imagine what he'd feel like if he came home and found her buried and his child gone?"

"We couldn't leave the baby and we couldn't stay to wait for anyone returning," Tempest protested.

"No. We can't leave her," Delia stated firmly. "And we won't."

"How old do you reckon she is?" Fairlee asked.

"Couple of months. She's filled out and has fat wrinkles on her legs and can almost hold her head up without wobbling. Remember when we first got to hold Martha

Jane?" Tempest said.

Delia nodded, smiling gently at the memory.

"Who?" Tyrell asked.

"Our cousins have children. Martha Jane is the oldest, and we weren't allowed to hold her until she was big enough to hold her head up. She was two months old when that happened," Delia explained.

"Well, this is March, so the baby's birthday should be in January," Fairlee said.

Tempest let the baby suck on the tip of the spoon after she'd swallowed the last bit of milk. "That sounds like a good birthday to me."

"What are you going to do with a baby?" Tyrell asked.

"Take her home to Aunt Rachel. Either she'll raise her, or one of the cousins' wives will take care of her. I expect Rosy will be in heaven over her. She's been saying that it's time for her to have more children to raise or she's no use anymore," Fairlee said.

"Rosy?" Isaac asked.

"That's our nanny. She's raised three generations of Lavalles."

"But that baby ain't a Lavalle," Isaac argued.

Fairlee glared at him. "She is now. Didn't you see those blue eyes? She'll fit right in."

Isaac shrugged and changed the subject. *Women and babies. It didn't do to argue with either.* He'd never understand them anyway. "You takin' first watch, Tyrell?"

"Yes, I will. One hour each until morning. Tempest, if the child starts to whimper, you see to it that she's fed and taken care of. You won't do watches because you'll be up and down with the baby. The rest of you had better get some sleep," Tyrell said.

Delia quietly unfurled her sleeping roll under a tree. She would offer to take care of the baby, but Hannah Marie Smith had taught her a valuable lesson. She'd wanted that little girl, and giving her up after only a day had broken her heart. She wasn't ready to bond with another child. Besides, Tempest was doing a fine job with her.

She was almost asleep when the fears set in. What if the Indians had seen their party of six and were following them until nightfall with plans of killing them all for their horses? What would happen to that poor little baby girl then?

She finally fell asleep, but her body was tense and her nightmares vivid. She awoke with a startled jerk when Micah touched her shoulder.

"It's an hour until dawn. You always like

the last watch so you can fix breakfast," he said.

"Anything going on?" she whispered.

"It's been quiet so far. I've heard tell that Indians often strike at this time of morning, when everything is still, so keep your eyes open. Want me to stay up with you?"

"No, go on and get another hour of rest." She removed her knife from its sheath and laid it on a nearby rock where she could easily reach it.

A deer ran through the trees so close that Delia could count the points on its antlers. The noise startled her, and her pulse throbbed. She willed it to settle down as she fried another skillet of bread and got out the leftover chicken and rabbit. There would be plenty for the morning meal. Lunch would be jerky again.

The bread had finished cooking when she tentatively touched Tyrell's shoulder.

"Breakfast's ready," she said softly.

He awoke quickly. "All quiet?" he asked.

She nodded.

"Baby?"

"Tempest fed her a couple of times in the night."

"Guess the cow's milk is agreeing with her, then?"

"It'll have to do until we get to Louisiana

and find her a wet nurse. Wake the rest of them. I'm as jittery this morning as a —" She stopped midsentence, before she said "new bride."

"It'll pass, the farther we get away from that burned-out place."

Delia didn't argue, but she didn't believe it. Her raw nerves weren't going to settle down until she got home. And then it might take ages before she felt safe again, after the sight of that poor woman wrapped around her child.

CHAPTER TWELVE

Knots of stress had settled into both sides of Delia's neck by the end of the day, but she rode without complaining. The only time she relaxed was when Tempest handed the baby over to her for a couple of hours. She hummed lullabies, and the baby looked up at her with big blue eyes. Someday Delia was going to have a whole houseful of children. They were going to have blue eyes and look exactly like the baby in her arms.

The sun had begun to disappear and the trees around them were dark with shadows when Tyrell noticed a thin spiral of smoke. "You all stay back in the shadows. I'm going to ride ahead. If it's a campsite, we'll circle it and go on. If it's Cherokee, we'll hide until they leave at daybreak. I'm hoping it's a farmhouse."

Delia pulled up her reins. Fairlee stopped beside her on her right, Tempest on her left. Isaac was in front of her, Micah behind them. An owl hooted in the distance, and a coyote answered. Delia only hoped it *was* a bird and a four-legged wild animal and not Cherokee hooting and howling messages. She had given the baby back to Tempie and had her hand on her knife when Tyrell returned.

"It's a farmhouse. I think we're safe to ride on in," he said.

Delia sighed when she saw a house and a barn. Goats and a few rangy cows were grazing in a corralled area not far from the house. Pigs were snorting and rooting around in a pen beyond the outhouse.

A lady stepped out onto the porch and shaded her eyes with one hand. She was tall and raw-boned with two long blond braids hanging down her chest. When they rode up into the yard, she smiled. "Y'all just passin' through or lookin' for a place to settle?"

"Passing through," Tyrell answered.

"Well, put the horses in the barn, and come on in. We got a pot of soup on the stove we'll be glad to share with you for a bit of news. We heard the Indians were raidin'. My husband, Thomas, is out in the barn," she said.

"We'd be obliged. Would you have any

cow's milk to sell us for the baby?" Delia asked.

The woman opened the door wide and held it for them. "No, but I've got lots of goat milk. It works just as well. The cows are about to come fresh, and they aren't producin' for us right now. We've been usin' goat milk a few weeks now. Let the menfolk take care of your stock, and you ladies come on inside. I ain't seen another woman in months. I'm dyin' for a little talk."

The log house was one big room divided by hand-hooked rugs. The left side was the bedroom area with a straw-stuffed mattress atop a bed frame with four tall posts. The right side was the kitchen, with an enormous stone fireplace where the soup pot hung. The aroma of fresh bread and cooking food and the light of two well-placed candles chased away the evening gloom.

"My name is Betsy Cunningham. My husband is Thomas. We've been here three years now, and the Indians have let us be, but there's always that fear that they'll raid again," she said.

"I'm Delia Lavalle. These are my sisters, Tempest and Fairlee."

"And which one of you has a new baby?"

Delia told the story of finding the child near the burned-out barn at a farm about ten or fifteen miles back down the road. "So the child doesn't belong to us, but we couldn't leave her to die," she explained.

"May I hold her please?" Betsy asked.

Tempest handed her over. "I reckon she's about two months old."

"I'm thirty-one and never been able to have children. Thomas and I wanted one so bad when we married twelve years ago, but they didn't come along. Would you consider leaving her with me?" Betsy asked.

That idea hit Fairlee like a welcome ice storm in the middle of a sweltering July. They hadn't even thought about finding the baby a new home.

"Delia? Tempest?" she said.

"I'd be a good mother," Betsy said. "I promise. I've always wanted a daughter more than anything in the world. I know this is hard country, but I'll protect her, and Thomas will too. You all think about it while you eat, and I'll rock her a spell if that's all right."

Tempest nodded. After only one day and night, she was worn out — up several times during the night, diapers to change and wash. Add that to feeding the baby with a spoon and hoping she was getting enough into the child to sustain her and yet not too fast for fear she'd choke the little thing to death.

Delia ladled out the soup for the three of them and uncovered a skillet of corn bread sitting in the middle of the rough-hewn table. The baby would have a safer, richer life at Oak View than what she was seeing in the log cabin, she reflected. She'd have fancy dresses and hair ribbons and a pony to ride. But Betsy Cunningham could give her a mother's love born of a true desire for a child.

Fairlee glanced at Betsy. She had an honest, hardworking face, and she'd been generous with her home and her food. Not at all like that ferryman's wife, who'd overcharged them for everything she'd shoved out the back door. She felt good about this woman and was about to say so when Thomas Cunningham ushered in the three men.

"Come right on in here and set at the table. Eat your fill. I know you've had a long day," he said.

He was a big blond man with the accent of a Swede. His hands were like bear paws, his face square. "What's that you got, Betsy? A baby? Which one of these gals is the mother?"

Betsy quickly told him the story. "And

195

they rescued the wee thing, Thomas," she concluded.

"My Betsy loves babies. Too bad God didn't see fit to give her a houseful. She'd have made a good mother," Thomas said.

He peered down into the center of the coat with the baby snuggled inside. He rubbed a calloused hand on her chubby little cheek, and she opened her eyes wide. "Why, look at that, Betsy. She's got big blue eyes, just like yours."

"Yes, but she's not got my rough old face. She's going to have a round face, more like yours, Thomas."

Thomas tickled the baby under the chin and got a grin for his efforts. "Well, she's a beauty, all right. Any man would be proud to call her his own, now, wouldn't he? It's too bad her own ma and pa won't never know that she survived and has these good people to care for her."

"Ah, but they will, Thomas. God wouldn't keep that from them. He'll be sure they know that their baby is well cared for," Betsy said.

"Yes, He will, Betsy." He patted his wife on the shoulder and turned his attention to the table, where Delia had poured soup for the men. "What news other than the Indian raid can you give us?"

"Everything else has seemed quiet. We were surprised to see that place burned out. Not even one Cherokee has shown his face. I'm sure they know we're passing through, but they haven't made themselves known," Tyrell answered.

"This is good soup," Micah said. He was tired of talking about Indians. He'd rather talk about food or anything else that didn't involve looking over his shoulder every thirty seconds and jumping every time the wind blew through the trees.

"Why, thank you, son. I had a feelin' this mornin' that I should make a big pot of it." Betsy continued to rock the baby.

Thomas laughed. "She gets those feelin's often. I think it's just hope that someone will drop by and give her a rest from the sound of my old voice."

"I was right this time, wasn't I?" Betsy said.

"That you was, my darlin'." He drew up a second rocking chair next to her and put his big finger into the baby's small hand. She wrapped her tiny fingers around his.

"So I'm wonderin', since the Indians haven't even been around here, if that raid on the farm mighta been someone else doin' it and makin' it look like the Indians."

"Could be," Tempest said thoughtfully.

"Can you remember anything about the arrows?" Thomas asked.

Isaac looked up. "There weren't any arrows. The woman was shot in the back."

"Well, some of the Indians have guns now, but most of them still use the bow. Could've been Indians for sure, but it could've been white men who wanted to rob the farm too," Thomas said.

"This is hard country, ain't it?" Micah said.

"To us it's good country for settlin'. Me and Betsy, we been here three years and ain't had no trouble. We're a far piece from anyone else, though, so maybe that's why they leave us be. You hear anything about Sam Houston goin' after old Santa Anna?"

"We left San Antonio on February twenty-third. Haven't heard much since except that the Mexicans were trying to starve out the Texans at the Alamo," Tyrell said.

"Well, we ain't seen no one but one man who come through in a big hurry to join up with Sam Houston to do some Mexican fightin'. So I guess Santa Anna is still on the prowl," Thomas said.

"Look at her, Thomas. She's sleepin' like an angel," Betsy said. She didn't care about battle rumors. She was as close to heaven as she could be right then without dying.

"If it would be all right with you all, we'll bed down in your barn," Tyrell said. "We'd be glad to pay for the food and lodging."

Thomas shook his head. "No, sir. The look on my Betsy's face is enough payment. Ain't often she gets women company or a baby to hold. You just go right on and use whatever you need in the barn. Breakfast will be ready long afore sunup so you can get a fresh start with a bellyful of food. We slaughtered a hog, and I shot a deer last week. We'll send along meat from the well house to last you a day or two."

Tempest looked at Delia, who nodded. Fairlee did the same.

"We've got a long journey ahead of us, and it could be dangerous," Delia said around a lump in her throat. She simply wouldn't tell Rosy about the baby they had almost brought home. "If you're still interested, I think you'd make a fine mother for that child, Betsy."

Betsy gasped, and tears spilled down her cheeks. "Thomas?"

Tears filled his eyes and rolled down his ruddy cheeks. "It's a miracle from God, Betsy."

"That it is, Thomas. What's your momma's name?" She looked at Delia.

"Our mother died last winter. Her name

was Rosetta Lavalle," Delia said.

"Then this baby girl is Rosetta Lavalle Cunningham, and we will remember you three women the rest of our lives. We'll tell her the story of how we came to be her parents when she's old enough to understand," Betsy said.

"Welcome home, little Etta," Thomas said softly.

They were on their way to the barn before Tyrell spoke up. "That was pretty unselfish of you all."

"Yes, it was," Delia said.

"Did you really want to keep that baby?" he asked her.

"I did. I love children," she told him.

"So do I," Tempest said honestly, "but I have to admit, I want a house to raise them in and a nanny to help. I'm so weary from one night of getting up and down from a bedroll that I could cry. I can't imagine how I'd feel in another two weeks."

They all crawled up the ladder to the loft, and the men took the left side. The women went to the right, and Tyrell sat down near the opening. He was relieved that they wouldn't have to be constantly on the lookout for milk for the baby, but a nagging little voice inside his head kept repeating

the words Delia had said: *I love children.*
She was twenty-one yet still unmarried. Did
she want to raise a family of her own but
hadn't found the right man? Would she be
willing to sacrifice her fancy style of life for
something simpler?

Delia took down her hair and combed it,
braided it into two long plaits that reached
her waist, and laid down, but sleep wouldn't
come. Had she done the right thing? Would
that baby have a chance in the wild Texas
frontier? She had to hope so. And what
about her? Would she ever have a blue-eyed
baby of her own?

All four of the younger folks were sleeping
soundly when Tyrell looked over his shoulder. He wasn't expecting to lock gazes with
Delia. He'd hoped to look his fill of her for
a while, to see her black lashes fanned out
across her fair cheeks, which were starting
to tan with so much sun. She'd have to soak
her face in buttermilk every night to get it
back to that translucent state he'd admired
when he first met her — back when she was
an angel of the Lord.

Delia sat up and crawled across the space
to him. "What is it? Is something the matter?"

She peered out the loft window, but the

countryside looked peaceful and calm. It was hard to believe there were any Indians within miles of the farm. Even the pigs and cows were quiet. The only noise was the soft rustle of the trees as a spring breeze flowed through their leaves.

"Nothing's wrong. I was just making sure everyone was all right before I turned in," he said softly.

"I couldn't sleep. We did make the right decision giving Betsy that baby, didn't we?"

He considered her question. "I think so. Fate seemed to put her into our care to bring to Betsy and Thomas."

"Tell me they're good folks," she pleaded.

"You don't need me to tell you that. You know it. You're just feeling guilty for leaving her here when you could have given her more at your home. But Betsy will dote on her, and so will Thomas. She will be loved and cherished."

"Thank you, Tyrell," Delia said softly.

"Want to sleep with me again?" he quipped.

"Don't ruin the moment," she scolded him.

"Then you'd best get on back to your chunk of hay, because I'm about to fall asleep," he said.

She turned to crawl back but got off balance, falling against him.

The next moment she was in his arms, and he was looking down at her, his lips coming closer and closer.

She tilted her chin to give him easier access and got ready for the jolt that would send tingles from toe to head when his mouth touched hers.

She was not disappointed. Except when it ended, and he said, "Good night, Delia."

"Why — why did you do that?"

"Did you like it? Did I do it right that time?" he teased.

"Oh, you! Good night, Tyrell." She crawled back to her place beside Fairlee.

It was a long time before she went to sleep. She kept wishing she could have dozed off cuddled up next to him like the last time.

CHAPTER THIRTEEN

Clouds hung low and a few sprinkles of rain kept the temperatures down the next day. Micah and Tempest had an argument, and Tempest rode alone behind Delia and Tyrell, grumbling the whole time about how she'd had enough of that man to last a lifetime and couldn't wait to get home so she never had to look at him again.

"How on earth Betsy Cunningham lives day after day after day with no one to talk to but a man is a mystery. If I had to live with you indefinitely, Micah," she told him during the noon break, "I'd put a knife in your liver and bury you under the outhouse."

"Stop your fighting," Fairlee said.

"Leave them alone. If they want to argue, it's their business, not yours," Isaac said.

Fairlee pointed a finger at him. "Don't you tell me what to do. I'm sick of their bickering. We've got days and days more to ride, and I don't want to listen to them slinging insults the whole time."

"You're just angry because you gave away that baby like a bag of chicken feed. It's not my fault you weren't women enough to keep her, so don't be mean to me for your decision," Isaac said.

Fairlee's eyes shot daggers at him. "We found her an excellent home and parents. We did not give her away like a bag of chicken feed!"

"You're right. You didn't. You sold her for a bowl of soup and a hot breakfast," he goaded her.

"You'd do well to stay away from me with your smart remarks." She went to a tree and plopped down behind it to finish her meal. *Danged men.* They'd never understand the sacrifice Delia, above all, had made when they let Betsy Cunningham have that child.

That afternoon Tempest and Fairlee rode together and whispered endlessly. Isaac and Micah brought up the rear and kept their eyes straight ahead, intent on getting the women home and lighting out for Mississippi.

"Familiarity appears to breed contempt," Tyrell commented to Delia.

She nodded. "That it does. Those four have been riding together for too long.

Throw any pairs of creatures together very long, and they're bound to have a disagreement or a fight. Look at what happened in the hotel that night. Tempie and Fairlee were about to tear up the place — until your sweetheart came onto the scene. Then they united because of blood."

"Who died and made you so smart?"

She shot him an evil look. "No one had to die to give me intelligence."

"Your sisters united 'because of blood'?"

"Think about it. You might fight with Isaac and Micah, but if someone else picked a fight with them, even though you were mad enough to whip both of them yourself, which side would you be on?"

"Family's, of course," Tyrell said.

"That's what I'm talking about. Tempie and Fairlee and I are united because we're kin. We can fight with each other, but even in the middle of the fight, we'd take up for one another," she explained.

"So why are they so touchy today?" he asked.

"They're tired of this travel. And they probably *aren't* convinced that we did the right thing leaving behind the baby when we could have given her more than those poor farmers can."

"And you?"

"I'll always wonder. But I know down deep that no one could love her more than those two people. She might not have a fancy house, but she'll have their undivided love and attention. So I'm glad we made the decision to leave her. Actually, it was tougher to leave Hannah behind," Delia said.

Tyrell frowned. "Why's that? You left her with natural parents and her brothers."

"I guess because I fought for her, risked my life for her, and fell in love with her. I had already had a chance to picture her blond curls bouncing as she skipped down the staircase in the house where we live. But it was a miracle that we met up with her parents," Delia said.

Tyrell didn't answer. Obviously Delia had gotten the common sense in the family. Most of the time the other two were spoiled brats. Well, that wasn't completely fair. They were all strong, caring women, but there was something extra special about Delia. . . .

"How much farther do we have to go?" Delia asked suddenly.

"With luck, about twenty miles tomorrow. With *lots* of luck and no bad weather to swell the creeks and Sabine River, maybe a week to your home. Three weeks, give or take a day, isn't bad for the kind of trip we've had. We were on the road a month chasing the man who killed Isaac and Micah's father, and that was riding without women."

" 'Without women'! That's so rude! We've ridden like men. We haven't complained. We've done our share." Her voice got shriller and higher.

Tyrell chuckled and threw up one hand, palm out. "Yes, you have, and I apologize for raising your hackles. This looks like a good place to make camp. Ready to stop for the night?"

"Yes," Delia said curtly.

They all slid off their horses and set about doing their nightly chores. Tempest commented that she missed having the mule to carry their provisions.

Micah pointed at her. "You know, I took care of that pack mule from the time we left the town where that little girl found her folks. You never did."

She glared at him. "I've done a better job than you the rest of the time, so don't be throwing that in my face. You are insufferable!" She stormed into the bushes, with Fairlee following her.

Micah threw up his hands and looked at Tyrell. "I see now why you never married. If they're all like this after a couple of weeks of being around them twenty-four hours a day, I'll never take a wife."

"Now you're getting smart," Isaac said.

Delia smiled. So Tyrell hadn't been married. Since it had taken an argument to find that out, she might have to start another one before the night was over to see if he had a prospective wife waiting in the wings.

She had set the skillet on the fire and was about to add grease to it when they heard screaming in the distance. She grabbed her knife and took off in the direction of the noise, all three men right behind her. If anyone wanted to steal their horses and their supplies, now would be the time, she thought vaguely as she ran.

"Delia, Tempie fell in a big hole, and she's not moving!" Fairlee yelled the minute she heard the thunder of running feet.

Delia grabbed Fairlee by the shoulders. "What are you talking about?"

Fairlee pointed at a deep pit in the ground. "We were walking, and she took a step, and she was gone. And now she won't talk to me. I think she's dead!" she moaned.

Micah peered down into the pit for only a second before he declared, "I'll get a rope and my horse. We'll get her out."

"Is she dead?" Fairlee cried.

"No, she's still breathing," Tyrell said. "I

think she's just knocked out. This is a trap for animals like mountain lions or raccoons. Their pelts bring pretty good money."

"Would you hush? We don't need a lesson in trapping. We need to get our sister out of that hole," Delia unfairly snapped at him.

Tyrell ignored her and studied the trap. The pit had been hidden with interlaced twigs and grass over the top. Whoever had made it evidently intended to catch something bigger than a mountain lion, a raccoon, or a coyote. The thing was big enough to trap a buffalo.

Micah brought his horse to the site and wrapped the rope firmly around the saddle horn. "I'll go on down there and bring her up. Whoever dug this thing must've been trying to trap elephants, as big as the hole is."

"Or a man," Isaac said grimly. Tyrell remained silent.

Delia jerked her head around to stare at Isaac. "Why would anyone want to capture a human being? Their hides wouldn't be worth anything."

"But what they've got on their hides and what they're riding on and what they're carrying to sustain their hides could be worth a lot. We could easily have a murderin' bandit just waitin' for all of us to eventually fall into the pit or else break a horse's leg, leaving us without anything to ride so he can catch us better," Isaac said.

"You're scaring me," Fairlee said, and Tyrell shot his cousin a quelling look.

Isaac nervously combed his dark hair with his fingers. It was too long by two months, and getting it cut when he got home was a priority, he thought absently. "Sorry," he grumbled.

Using the rope to rappel down the sides of the hole, Micah was soon at the bottom. He gently picked up Tempest and motioned for the others to bring them back up. Tyrell backed the horse up, and Micah used his strong arms to hold Tempest close to his chest. She was breathing, and he saw no major cuts or bruises, so most likely she'd be all right.

Delia came close to fainting when Tempest and Micah got out of the hole. She could see that Tempie had been lying atop a pile of bones, and that certainly did not look like a raccoon skull down there. If those weren't human teeth in that bleached-out head, Delia would be surprised.

"I was right," Isaac said self-righteously, then quieted when he saw Fairlee shiver.

Once she was safe back at Oak View, Fairlee vowed silently again, she would never leave. If her father could only come home to see them every couple of years, she'd learn to deal with it. She'd be satisfied to live right there the rest of her life.

Delia was on the ground, cradling Tempest's head in her arms. "Wake up, sister. Please wake up," she whispered, tears in her eyes.

Tempie's eyelids fluttered, and she awoke with a jerk that went from her head to her toes. "What — what happened?"

"You fell into a trapper's hole," Delia said.

Tempest made no move to sit up but shut her eyes tightly, then snapped them back open. "There were skeletons in there, and they were grabbing at me!"

Micah wrapped the rope around his arm and put it back on the saddle horn. "In those seconds of your fall, I bet those dried-up bones down there did look like they were grabbing at you. You sure got the wind knocked out of you. Are you certain you aren't hurt or something is broken? Can you walk?"

"Of course I can walk." Tempest sat up and waited until everything stopped spinning. She'd never admit that she was dizzy. Not after all the comments the men had made about women.

She slapped her hat back onto her head

with enough force to show them all she was angry at the suggestion that she couldn't walk. Then she stood and headed back toward the campsite.

"Whoa, wait a minute. Not so fast," Tyrell said.

Tempest stopped so fast that the dizziness and her forward momentum almost sent her flying headlong. "What? I can walk. I'm fine. I wouldn't want to slow you down," she said sharply.

"That's not the point," Tyrell said mildly.

He picked up a long branch. "There could be more than one trap, and the grass on top of that one was very fresh. It hasn't been there more than a day — two at the most — or it would have been dried up. Micah, follow me with my horse, and the rest of you come along single file."

He chose the path they'd taken when they ran toward Fairlee's scream. He poked the ground in a wide circle and took another step, repeating the process over and over until they were all back at the camp.

"Are we going to have to do that tomorrow when we leave here?" Delia's hands shook when she started preparing supper.

"I'll walk ahead for the first mile or two, and we'll go slowly. I think after that we'd probably be safe. Whoever is doing this is banking on folks crossing the creek and making camp right there in that perfect spot," Tyrell said.

"I can't sleep thinking about it. Let's move on tonight," Delia said.

"We got an hour of light left, Tyrell. We could be out of the area by dark if we hurried up with supper," Isaac said.

"Tempest?" Tyrell asked.

She brushed dirt from her shirt, but the memory of those bones reaching for her didn't go away. "I'd just as soon be as far away from here as possible."

"You've had a fall. You might want to rest," he suggested.

She set her jaw. "I can keep up with you boys anytime, night or day."

"Okay, then, we'll eat as we ride. Put the cooking pan away, and rustle up some leftovers, please, Delia," Tyrell said.

It was slow going, but by dark they'd covered at least half a mile. Tyrell had discovered several more traps, some deep enough to hobble a horse. Some could have held a small animal, and two could have easily held a human. None of them had bones in them, however, and they were all covered with fresh grass. Tyrell wished there was some way he could warn anyone riding behind them about the danger, but he had no idea how to do it other than to uncover the holes and make them visible.

"There's going to be some almighty mad trappers when they find their pits all uncovered," Delia said.

"If we had time to spare, we'd fill them all in with rocks," he replied.

Tyrell Fannin is a good man, Delia thought. *It's his goodness that made me fall in love with him.*

She sat up very straight in her saddle and looked around to see if anyone had read her mind. Good grief, what had made her even think such a thing? *Tyrell* and *love* in the same sentence? It couldn't be, could never happen. He might have kissed her twice and sent shock waves through her body, but . . . love? Besides, even though he wasn't married, he might have already picked out a woman back in Mississippi.

I have no right to be jealous. Those two kisses, one of which was nothing but a reaction because I fell against him, were not promises of any kind. But I am jealous, so I'll admit it and work hard to get over it. Maybe by the time he's gone from my life and out of my sight for a few weeks — months? years? — I will forget him.

She shook her head. It wasn't likely that she'd ever forget Tyrell Fannin or this trip with the "outlaws." Mercy, but she'd thrown a fit about starting out with a bunch of low-lifes fresh out of jail as guides and protection. She'd been the biggest crybaby of the three of them the day her father told them to pack for a trip, that they would be leaving in an hour.

Fairlee had stomped her feet, folded her arms over her chest, and refused to pack. Tempest had been ready to do whatever her father thought best — until he mentioned the nuns' habits. At that point, she'd pitched a temper tantrum. She wasn't going anywhere dressed like a nun. If she couldn't ride a horse, then she wasn't going. She'd stay and fight the Mexicans at the Alamo.

But Tempie and Fairlee had been shocked speechless when Delia stood up to their father and declared that God might strike them all dead for impersonating nuns, that no one on the face of the entire earth could be further removed from an angel of God than the Lavalle sisters.

Still, Captain Lavalle wouldn't be swayed, and Delia had sobbed bitterly at being forced to leave him to his fate at the Alamo.

And God hadn't tossed lightning from heaven toward three nuns who wore trousers and boots under their habits, who had saddles and guns in their wagon. Luck or

God, or a combination of the two, and three Mississippi men had brought them safely through every ordeal, including the trap that Tempie had fallen into that evening.

Micah rode up to the front of the line. "How much longer we going to ride?"

Tyrell shrugged. "You getting tired?"

"Not really. Might as well stay at it a while longer if the womenfolk ain't too weary. Moon is giving good light. Clouds have blown on out toward the northeast. The more miles we can put between us and the trappers, the better I'd feel," he said.

"Don't you be worryin' your head none about us," Tempest said from behind Delia. "We can go as long as you can. Besides, it's going to be a long time before I can shut my eyes and not see skeletons grabbin' at me."

Tyrell nodded off in the saddle a couple of times but had gotten a second wind at daybreak when they found a settlement on the west side of the Sabine River. Huge boats were lined up waiting to be loaded with merchandise to carry south down the river. When the cotton came in in the fall, the riverbank would be even more crowded.

Tyrell found the nearest hotel and rented two rooms. The clerk asked if they would be interested in baths, and he bought six. They had breakfast in the dining room, with other female guests looking down their noses at the women in pants and men's shirts. Little did they know that, in Tyrell's opinion, the Lavalle women were made of sturdy stock but would probably look better in dresses than they did.

After they'd eaten, the three men carried their clean clothing to the bathing quarters in a back room of the hotel. Tubs were lined up against a wall, filled with steaming water. Drying sheets and bars of soap waited on chairs beside each tub, along with a cigar, a metal ashtray, and a lit candle.

They each claimed a tub and slid down into the warm water, letting it ease the tension from their weary muscles. They bit the end off the cigars, lit them by the candle flame, and soaked in the tubs until the water was cold.

In the ladies' bathroom, tubs lined the wall but were sectioned off with privacy curtains around each. Drying sheets, bars of soap, and a bottle of sweet-smelling oil awaited each customer.

Delia dropped her dirty clothing to the floor along with her boots and purred like a kitten when she sank down into the water. She wasn't getting out until her skin looked like a dried apricot.

"So, are you ready to admit that you're attracted to Tyrell Fannin?" Tempest asked from the other side of the curtain.

"I am not," she declared.

"Might as well. It's written all over your face," Fairlee said from her cubicle.

"It is not. You two just want me married off so the old-maid sister will be out of the way for you. Well, let me tell you something. I may never marry, so you might as well start chasing the fellows of your choice, and let me be the old maid who's a little crazy and names her rosebushes," Delia said.

"Pretty long speech. I'd say she's protesting too much, Fairlee," Tempest said.

"Me too. But let's give it another week and see if she pouts when Tyrell rides away from the plantation," Fairlee said.

"Have you ever in your lifetime felt anything as wonderful as this bath? And just think, we have big old soft beds waiting for us when we finish. I'm going to sleep like a baby," Delia said.

"Yep, she's talkin' too much and changing the subject. She's going to wither away to nothing when he leaves us at the plantation," Tempie said.

Delia had a smart remark on the tip of her tongue, but she bit it back. She would never wither away to nothing for any man.

She might whimper, but her sisters would darn sure never hear it.

CHAPTER FOURTEEN

The sun was setting rather than rising when Delia opened her eyes. She wriggled down into the mattress and tried to will herself to go back to sleep. She adjusted her pillow, untangled her legs from the sheets. Nothing worked. Finally she sat up, pushed back the quilt, and looked for Tempest and Fairlee. Neither was in the bedroom. The sounds from a dozen saloons mingled and drifted in the open window. She wrapped the quilt around her body and stepped out onto the balcony. The river town was coming to life. Conversations, both muted and heated, found their way to her ears as she sat down on a straight-backed chair. The aroma of bacon, beans, and yeasty bread filled her nose, and her stomach growled.

She scanned the street up and down, checking for cafes or restaurants. Then she heard Fairlee and Tempie's voices right below her on the hotel's front porch.

221

"That was the best steak I've eaten since we left home," Tempie said.

"We should have awakened Delia. Now she'll have to eat alone," Fairlee said.

"Why don't we take food up to her? We can surprise her."

"She could eat on the balcony. Remember when we were little girls and Momma would let us take our supper out on the upstairs porch in the spring?"

Tempie giggled. "I can almost smell home, Fairlee."

Tempest's laughter was prettier than the finest harp music at a Sunday afternoon social to Delia that night. And they were nearing home. Things were changing from one day to the next, and that morning, when they'd neared the river town, Delia had actually seen a bit of moss hanging from a live oak. Soon they'd be back in Louisiana; soon Tempest would laugh more and frown less. Soon Tyrell would be out of her life and she could stop thinking about him every waking moment and then dreaming about him when she slept.

She was still sitting on the balcony when her sisters brought the "surprise."

"Oh, my!" she exclaimed. "What a wonderful, thoughtful treat!"

"We woke up an hour ago and were hungry, but we decided to let you sleep." Tempie sat on the edge of the bed and talked through the open door.

"This is a wonderful steak. It could have come straight out of Fanny's kitchen," Delia said.

"That's what I said. So what do we do now?" Tempest asked. "I'm wide awake, and it's nighttime. What do ladies do when they've slept all day and can't sleep at night? Our laundry won't be back until morning, or we could ride all night and get home quicker."

"I'm going to sit here and watch the people. I don't even care if they're saloon girls and brawling drunks. It's good to hear voices and look at something other than trees," Delia said.

"Not me. I'm going to go right back to bed and sleep until morning. My body isn't ever going to get enough rest," Fairlee said.

"Safe rest," Delia said.

"What do you mean by that?" Tempest asked.

"Our bodies feel this tired because even when we sleep on the trail, it's not safe rest. We won't get safe rest until we get home. Did you see the moss today?" Delia asked.

"I did," Fairlee said. "I almost fell off my horse and kissed the dirt. We have to be getting close to home. I've decided to take your advice and marry within the year, Delia. I'm going to find a beau and settle down. I never want another adventure."

"I do," Tempest said. "I want to travel some more, but by stage and where it's safe. Where there're no trappers or Indians to scare the devil out of me. How about you, Delia?"

She thought about the question. "I don't know. We haven't made it home yet."

Tempest yawned. "I believe I *could* sleep again. Must be the good food. Y'all talk a little louder so I can hear you while I'm dozing off. It'll seem more like home that way. Remember when we were little girls and shared a room? I always loved it when you two would talk until I went to sleep. I was convinced the bogey man wouldn't get me if someone was awake."

"Honey, if the bogey man did get you, he would have brought you home pretty quick. Even Lucifer couldn't live with a Lavalle for long. It took a saint like Momma to live with Father," Delia said, silently hoping and praying that he was all right. Her sisters seemed eager to talk about him too, as if that would mean he was safe.

"Maybe it took Father being gone for months at a stretch for them to stay together. They both had hot tempers, and every time he was home for more than a month, they clashed horns. They might not have gone the distance on a full-time basis," Fairlee said.

"Maybe *I* should marry a military man," Delia joked.

"Already giving up on Tyrell?" Fairlee teased.

"Go to bed, and don't start that again."

Fairlee smiled. "Yes, ma'am. Don't fall asleep out here. It might get colder during the night, and you'll catch a chill."

Delia called to her sister through the open door. "If I didn't catch a chill sleeping on the ground, I doubt I'd get one out here with a quilt wrapped around me."

In a few minutes she heard her sisters' soft inhaling and exhaling. Then the saloon noise got louder. Piano music made its way up and down the street. Delia wondered what it would be like to walk into a saloon, order a nice brandy, and sit at a table to listen to the music. The closest she'd ever been to such a thing was the morning after they'd rented the upstairs rooms in a saloon, and she'd visited with the piano player.

Delia played the piano and the harp and was sought after at socials in her area. She

225

shut her eyes and envisioned herself in a fancy dress that stopped at her knees and showed the ruffles of her pantaloons, her hair piled high with a red feather anchored in it. Would that kind of getup make Tyrell Fannin see her as a desirable woman? Or would he always see a nun or a woman in trousers without a single feminine trait?

She drew her chair closer to the railing, propped up her elbows, and put her chin in her hands. The saloon she could see the best was diagonally across the street. Two men sat on a bench in front of the swinging doors, their hats drawn low on their brows. They looked familiar, but she didn't know anyone in the town they were in.

She did know the man who swaggered out of the swinging doors. Without a doubt in the world, that was Tyrell Fannin, and it didn't take a genius to know what kind of woman was hanging on his arm. The light from the saloon lit up her bright pink dress, which was cut low and off her shoulders. Part of her red hair was pinned up, and the rest lay in curls down her back to her waist. Her skirt didn't come close to covering her knees, and the lace on her petticoats showed with every step she sashayed alongside Tyrell.

Delia's first thought was to get dressed

and snatch a handful of red hair off that brazen woman's head. Her second was to get her gun and dust up the dirt around her fancy boots and Tyrell's worn ones. Her third was that it was none of her business and good for her to realize that she'd had him on a pedestal since she'd figured out she was in love with him. Well, that could dang well change in a hurry. He'd only been nice to her because it was his job to do so. What really caught his eye was a loose woman who would never worry him about standing in front of a preacher.

The two men who'd been sitting on the bench stood up, and she realized they were Isaac and Micah. Tyrell said something to the woman, probably making arrangements for later, slapped his cousins on the back, and walked across the street. None of them looked up at the balcony and saw her.

She scooted her chair back and seethed. There was no way she could sleep again until she sorted out her feelings. She was still seething when she felt a presence beside her and jerked her head around to find Tyrell pulling a chair from the door to his bedroom. The glow of his cigar was a red dot in the darkness, and the smoke smelled sweet, like the library after Uncle Jonathan and his cronies had after-dinner drinks.

"Figured you'd sleep until morning," he said.

"You figured wrong," she snapped.

"Wake up on the wrong side of the bed, or have you not eaten yet?"

"Neither one. I slept well, and my sisters brought me food. I finished a wonderful steak a while ago," she said.

"Then it must be the company. What did I do now?"

She tried to form words that wouldn't give away her feelings, but they wouldn't come. She looked straight ahead and ignored him.

"This is the best hotel in town. You had a bath, and the rooms are excellent. What put you in such a bad mood?" he persisted.

"Maybe this is my normal mood, and it's just now surfacing since we're drawing near to home."

Tyrell sucked in cigar smoke and looked down at the saloon. The red-haired girl named Devine opened the swinging doors and stepped out for a breath of fresh air with another man. He hugged her up close to his side and kissed her on the neck. She giggled and slapped at his arm. Likely she told him she'd be available later that night if he'd come back at closing time and gave him her price.

Tyrell could have recited her words verbatim because it had only been a few minutes since he'd heard them. The only difference was that he hadn't kissed her on the neck. Every time he saw a redhead, he thought of Lucy Adams, the woman who'd run off with another man after she'd promised to marry him. All women were beyond understanding, but red-haired ones were the worst of the lot when it came to trusting.

He looked across the distance separating him and Delia. The soft candlelight from the hotel room cast a glow on her profile as she stared straight ahead. Her chin was tilted upward, and the muscles of her jaw worked in anger. A fork and knife were crossed on an empty plate set on a chair on the other side of her. She'd been on the balcony long enough to eat supper. She was wrapped in a quilt, which said she had come out there right after she awoke.

"So, you been out here long?"

"Long enough."

"Guess you saw that woman escorting me out of the saloon, didn't you?"

"What's that got to do with anything?"

"She offered me a night in her room over the saloon for the right price. I'd just have to go back after hours," he said.

Delia held her hands tightly under the quilt. She couldn't slap him. She had no right. What he did was his business except when he was protecting her and her sisters on the trip. He was right. He'd found them a wonderful hotel complete with a bathroom and good food.

"I told her I wasn't interested," he said.

Her hands relaxed slightly, and the blood flowed back into her white knuckles.

Tyrell went on. "I was engaged once several years ago. Her name was Lucy Adams. She was a red-haired girl, and I fancied myself in love with her. She said she'd marry me, then eloped with another man. Redheads. They might be nice. They could be good, hardworking, decent women, but honey, I don't intend to ever form any type of relationship with a redhead," he said mildly.

He smoked his cigar, and the noise from the saloon overpowered the taverns down the street. A river town had enough trade to support several saloons, and they competed with one another for business. It had shocked Delia to learn that women actually propositioned men in that way. She wasn't so naïve that she didn't know about saloon girls and what went on in the rooms upstairs, but she'd imagined the men did the asking.

"You're not engaged now?" she ventured.

230

Tyrell practically choked. "Hell, no! Pardon my language. If I had a woman waiting for me, I wouldn't have kissed you — twice. Hell, I wouldn't have kissed you at all. I would never do that to a woman I'd asked to marry me. I'd be a faithful husband if I'm ever one at all."

Delia's fingers unwound themselves from one another, and she drew the quilt closer to her chest. That had been easy enough. What else could she find out about Tyrell Fannin?

"You? Is there someone you've got your eye on back home?" Tyrell held his cigar perfectly still while he waited for the answer.

"No. Had a couple of offers, but I didn't love them," she said honestly.

"You think love and marriage should go hand in hand?" he asked.

"If they don't, I won't have either," she told him.

"Folks marry for reasons other than love," he pointed out.

"Not me. I can't imagine living with a person every day for the rest of my life without love. You know, this is a strange conversation, Mr. Fannin. It's pretty liberal for an unmarried woman and man to be sitting in the dark with no chaperone and talking about such things," she said.

"Yes, it is, but I'm your bodyguard, not your paramour, so that makes it all right."

Delia turned to look at him. "My Aunt Rachel would disagree. I'm wrapped in a quilt watching women of the night you've been talking to. I think that might well be considered improper."

"I expect it is. I'll leave you to your evening, then."

Oddly unwilling to make her uncomfortable in the least, he reluctantly left the chair and went back into his room, shutting the door softly behind him.

Micah and Isaac were sitting on the edge of one bed with a deck of cards.

"We're playin' a little poker to see if it will bore us to sleep. Want to join us?" Isaac asked.

Tyrell crushed the end of his cigar in a glass tray on the washstand. "No, thanks. I'm going to bed. We'll have a long day tomorrow. I'd like to cross over into Louisiana before we stop. If I remember right, there's a town there that has a hotel. Then the next night we should be closing in on the Lavalles' place. Three days, tops, and we can leave the women behind and make better time getting home."

"Hallelujah!" Isaac said. "I'm never crossing the state line again. I'll be a Mississippi man until the day I die — and happy to be so."

"Amen to that," Micah said. "But how 'bout you, Tyrell? Can you leave Delia Lavalle behind that easily and just forget her?" he asked.

"You goin' to weep and moan over Tempest?" Tyrell countered.

"Good God man, where did that come from? If I cried a tear over Tempest, it would be because we couldn't get rid of her right fast enough," Micah said.

Isaac tossed his cards onto the bed. "Full house. You owe me a hundred dollars."

"Take it off what you owe me," Micah teased.

"How much do you each have?" Tyrell asked.

"I'm up about a million. He's only got a few thousand," Micah said.

"Havin' a bad night," Isaac said. "I'll win it all back later."

"That's what the gamblers who use real money say," Tyrell told him.

"I'm too tight-fisted to use real money. That's why I only gamble with pretend money and only with Isaac or you," Micah said.

Tyrell stretched out on the other bed. "Good night."

"You didn't answer my question," Micah said.

"Don't intend to answer it."

He shut his eyes, and in a few minutes he was asleep. As usual, Delia haunted his dreams — and she was not wearing men's clothing or riding a horse.

CHAPTER FIFTEEN

Delia was excited at the prospect of getting home in two days. They would stay at a hotel later that evening as they crossed the border from Texas into Louisiana. The next night they would be at Bennett's Bluff among friends, and the following afternoon they'd be at Oak View.

On the other hand, the idea of the journey's end made her blue. She'd had the adventure of a lifetime to tell her children and grandchildren. But Tyrell would be gone from her life, never to be seen again. That part made her want to rein in her horse, sit still under the oak trees dripping with moss, and stop their progress right there.

Both parts made her cranky. She tried to think about spring bringing the rebirth of new life, rather than the ending of a trip and the odd, guarded friendship she'd formed with Tyrell Fannin. Nature created splashes of color all around them. Wildflowers of every shape, size, and color covered the ground. Blossoms graced the trees, and new growth proved that spring was definitely coming. There would be more chilly mornings, and the temperatures at night would drop, but the days, for the most part, would be sunny and nice. The garden would be planted when they returned. Before long they'd have fresh radishes and green beans.

Thinking about those simple pleasures lasted five minutes, and then she went back to the friendship-with-Tyrell idea. Friends didn't kiss each other the way Tyrell had kissed her, and friends didn't get jealous when a saloon girl offered a night in her bedroom. She and Tyrell Fannin had become more than friends. Admitting it was difficult; doing anything about it was impossible.

Tyrell looked ahead to spring with mixed feelings. He wanted to be home to help tend the cotton crop. Their foreman, Benjamin, could see to it that the work was done without them, but Tyrell missed the honest labor. He got up early every morning and spent the entire day right alongside his servants.

His father had taught him that work ethic

by example. *Never treat anyone, especially those people for whom you are responsible, with any less dignity than you'd want to be treated,* had been his motto. His Uncle Rural had been cut from the same cloth as his father.

The brothers-in-law had been friends all through their growing-up years. Then Jacob Fannin married Rural Burnet's sister, and they traveled to Mississippi together to claim the land they'd been granted. Two years later Rural fell in love with a neighbor woman, and they were married.

Jacob's wife — Rural's sister — died of fever when Tyrell was ten days old. Jacob hired a wet nurse and never married again. Cholera got him when Tyrell was eighteen. His Uncle Rural and Aunt Allie, along with Isaac and Micah, shared the land he'd inherited upon the death of his father. The younger boys had grown up at Tyrell's house as much as they had at home. And Tyrell ate as many meals at his Uncle Rural's house as he had at his own place. Then Aunt Allie got a fever and died a week later. Rural hadn't been the same after she was gone, and he'd spend days on end at an old cabin up in the woods at the far edge of the farm. It was there that they found him shot in the back. Truth of the matter was, it was probably where he would have wanted to die. It was where he and Allie first took up housekeeping, back before they built their home down near the center of the farm.

Tyrell, Isaac, and Micah had ridden out the afternoon after Rural's funeral. James Durran, the bandit who killed him, had a three-day head start, but he was riding Rural's horse, and that made him easier to track. It would be strange going home to their place without Rural. Tyrell suddenly felt old, thinking about filling the boots left behind.

He stole a glance at Delia, riding beside him. A man would have to be blind or downright stupid not to be attracted to a remarkable woman like her, with those light blue eyes and her take-charge attitude. But Delia Lavalle deserved someone with a lot more to offer than a Mississippi cotton farmer.

Tyrell sighed and attempted to think more about next fall's cotton crop and less about Delia.

Isaac kept his eyes straight ahead and off the woman who'd been riding beside him for days on end. Fairlee Lavalle was a pretty woman, for sure, but not someone he'd ever fancy. Isaac had the notion that when his real angel fell from heaven, she'd have long blond hair and big brown eyes. And she'd be a soft-spoken, delicate creature. She sure wouldn't wear men's trousers and ride anything other than sidesaddle, and she wouldn't be able to skin a rabbit or ride twenty or more miles a day without fainting.

He shook ideas of women from his head and thought about home. His father wouldn't be there. It hadn't really sunk in until that morning. His father was truly dead. Three days after they'd buried him, they were on the trail hunting down his murderer. Then there was that brawl in the San Antonio cantina. They'd been minding their own business when a Mexican stormed inside and accused Tyrell of flirting with his wife the night before.

Tyrell had told the man that he'd only gotten into town that day and was leaving to go back to Mississippi the next morning. The Mexican had slammed a fist into Tyrell's face. Too bad the Mexican fellow didn't know that Tyrell had a temper, and that temper had been cheated out of punishing the man who'd killed his uncle.

Then there were the Mexican's two companions, who wanted to help out their friend. Isaac and Micah couldn't let that happen. Before long everyone in the cantina wanted to get in a few slugs, but they were the only three who'd wound up in jail.

He glanced over at Fairlee. The man who wed that woman had better be ready to give up the pants in the family, figuratively and literally. Isaac felt a pang of sympathy for the unsuspecting fool. She would probably look like an angel when she was all dressed up, and the fellow would think he was getting someone with a halo and wings. But Isaac Burnet knew better. Poor man would be getting a devil in disguise.

Fairlee was antsy that morning. She wanted to be home, not just going in that direction. She hadn't even wanted to leave in the first place. The previous winter, when their mother died and Delia came up with the harebrained idea that they go comfort their father, Fairlee had protested for days.

Fairlee wondered as she rode alongside Isaac Burnet if Delia hadn't just wanted an adventure before she settled down and accepted one of the many offers of marriage that had come her way.

There was Andrew Trudeaux, who lived down in New Orleans and came to Oak View a couple of times a year to do cotton business with Uncle Jonathan. Then there was Samuel Leblanc, the entrepreneur in Lafayette, who owned a riverboat operation. Both men were wealthy and interested in a wife of Delia's standing and reputation.

Of course there was also Matthew Cheval over on the next plantation. At the spring parties and the Sunday socials he'd come around casting his eyes toward Delia. Fairlee had seen it and was a little jealous. Maybe if Delia was nice to Andrew or Samuel, then Matthew would look at her. He was a pretty young man with smooth skin, dark hair, and big brown eyes, and he always dressed so nice. Not that she was in love with the man, but he would make a fine husband.

She looked over at Isaac, who was staring rudely at her. "What do you want?"

"To be home and away from you," he said.

"I assure you, Mr. Burnet, the feeling is mutual," she said.

"What about Tyrell and Delia? You think they're eager for this trip to be over?" Isaac asked.

"I can't speak for my sister. She thinks on her own. But if I ever get home, I'm never leaving again," she said.

"I'm never leaving Mississippi again either," Isaac said.

■ ■ ■ ■

Tempest let her mind wander. She'd over-heard the few words exchanged by Isaac and Fairlee. She wasn't completely in agreement with what Fairlee had said. She wanted more adventures. Definitely not any as dangerous as the one they'd just experi-enced. But at least she wanted to travel to New Orleans and visit her mother's sister again, to giggle with her cousins like they were schoolgirls.

But they are all four married, she reminded herself with a sigh. They'd grown up, and so had she. She'd be expected to take a husband before long — probably should have already. But Delia had wanted to go to San Antonio to comfort their father, and that had put all courting on hold for a few months. Tempest had entertained ideas of a handsome soldier in her father's company who would catch her eye, but Captain La-valle had kept his daughters so sheltered, they hadn't met any of the military men who'd been sent to the Alamo. Now she could only hope those men were soldiers strong and true, defending the Alamo alongside her courageous father.

Looking back, she wondered if Delia had

been simply trying to run from the inevitable. They'd lived at Oak View their whole life. Her father had been raised there with his brother, Jonathan. When their parents died, the land was left to them equally. Robert had met Rosetta when he was stationed in New Orleans and brought her home to northern Louisiana Territory to his family home. She had stayed, and he had left for months, sometimes years, at a time.

That they had three daughters so close in age was due to the fact that he'd been home three times during those years. Rosetta had lost three other children after Tempest was born. One was stillborn. One lived a month and died in his sleep. The last one lived two days before he died.

Guess God didn't intend for her to raise a son, only to watch him go off to fight wars like her husband did, Tempest thought sadly.

Micah turned in the saddle often and checked their back trail, making sure no one was sneaking up on them. It would be terrible to get this close and be ambushed — or have to prolong their time with the Lavalle women.

He liked Delia the best out of the three, but he wouldn't shed tears at leaving her behind when they said good-bye. The Lavalles had all pulled their weight, but he wouldn't agree to a repeat trip even if the women were really nuns and Captain Lavalle laid *five* hundred dollars in gold in their hands.

He should have known the first time he heard Tempest giggle that she wasn't an angel of God. Nuns wore serious expressions and were always, always stern. They didn't resemble the Lavalle sisters in the least, with all that black hair, blue eyes, and the soft, giggling accent that sounded like honey mixed with a little bourbon to cut the sweetness. Their kind of women didn't become nuns, and he, his brother, and cousin should have seen that from the beginning. If they hadn't been so eager to get out of that jail, maybe they would have. Chalk the whole thing up to the Mexican who'd started the fight in the cantina. If it hadn't been for him, they wouldn't have been in jail. If they hadn't been in jail, they wouldn't have met Captain Robert Lavalle. Micah wished he had his hands firmly around that Mexican's neck right then. It was all his fault.

They stopped at an inn in a small border town that evening. It wasn't nearly as nice as the one they'd had the night before

244

they'd crossed the Sabine River, but the beds were clean. The clerk rustled them up a platter of cold meat, bread, and cheese, and they ate at a corner table in a small dining area.

"I'm thinking we'll be close to your place by tomorrow night," Tyrell said.

"We should be at Bennett's Bluff. We can spend the night there. They'll be glad for the company, and they're friends of the family," Delia said.

"Could they take you on home? We could leave you and get on our way," Isaac said bluntly.

"We'll finish the job we were paid for," Tyrell told him. "Are you sure this family would welcome three unknown men into their home?" he asked Delia.

"They will welcome any friends of ours," Delia said. There was that word — *friends* — again. She no longer knew what to think of Tyrell Fannin. "I'm taking my coffee up to the room. I'll see you all in the morning."

Tempest pushed back her chair. "You'll see *us* right now."

Fairlee stood up, and they trooped up the stairs, single file, in order of birth, leaving the men to their after-dinner cigars and talk.

■ ■ ■ ■

"I'm not so comfortable about stayin' in a fancy house with a name like that. It's probably one of those huge places we passed on our way through Louisiana. We don't even have the clothes," Isaac said.

"We are who we are. We're honest, hardworking men, and if we are asked to stay, we will. It'll save us the price of a hotel or sleeping on the ground. We have clean things in our saddlebags. We can certainly present ourselves as cotton farmers," Tyrell said.

"You're just wanting to see Delia in a dress," Micah said.

"You see a dress floating out of her saddlebags at any time?"

"No, but those people probably have trunkfuls she can borrow," Isaac said.

Tyrell shook his head slowly. "I doubt it. She's probably too proud to borrow. Tempest might not be, though. You might get to see *her* in a dress."

Micah spun around in his chair to look at Tyrell. "Don't tease me about that woman. I wouldn't want to see her in nothing."

Isaac chuckled under his breath. "Now, *that* might be interesting. Tempest in nothing."

Micah blushed so deeply that Tyrell laughed. "Don't let those women hear you saying that. They'd kill you in your sleep. What's the matter with you, Micah? Thinking about a nun with nothing on."

Micah frowned. "Hey, what was under those habits dang sure wasn't nuns. And what we've been riding with since then ain't nuns. But, just to be clear, I wouldn't want to see nuns *or* Tempest with nothing on. I just want to get them out of our hair and get back to our life."

Tyrell abruptly changed the subject. "I'm going to miss Uncle Rural. He kind of got to where he spent a lot of time up at the cabin the last few months, but he knew cotton like the back of his hand. Y'all reckon we learned enough to run the place?"

Isaac spoke around the lump in his throat. "I'm twenty-three. That's the age Papa was when he brought our mother home to be his wife. You're twenty-eight, Tyrell, and you've been shouldering a man's responsibility for years. Micah is twenty-two. We're not boys anymore. We've been trained, and we know the business of running a place the size of ours. Papa never called it a plantation, but it is one, you know."

"Just without the big fancy house," Micah said.

"I'd say our places are fancy enough. They're fine, two-story homes built on sturdy foundations," Tyrell said.

"I'm just glad the trip is about done," Micah said.

"I'm even glad your papa's murderer was dead when we got there. I'd have called him out, but looking back, I guess it all worked out the way it was supposed to," Tyrell mused aloud.

"Not me. If I had it to do over again, I would have hog-tied you and Isaac and never let you go into that cantina for a drink. I would have insisted we start home the minute we found that sorry fool Durran was dead," Micah said.

"Why?" Isaac asked.

"We would already be home, and we wouldn't have ever met those Lavalle sisters," Micah told him.

Tyrell didn't share Micah's opinion that they'd have been better off never to have met the Lavelles. Delia had made him see that some women *could* be trusted. He had finally moved past his fiancée's rejection. He wasn't sure when or where he had cut the chains loose from his heart, but he had, and he was ready once again to take a wife and raise a family.

CHAPTER SIXTEEN

They got an early start the next day and kept going through the noon meal stop. They came upon the turn to Bennett's Bluff at suppertime, and Delia reined in her horse.

"Why are we stopping?" Tempest asked.

"Because we can go on to Bennett's Bluff, or we can keep riding and be in our own beds by bedtime," Delia said.

"Then let's go home," Fairlee said. "I'm not so sure I want Mavis to see me lookin' like this anyway. She and Momma often disagreed on the way we were raised. She might not let us sit at her table wearing trousers."

"Tempest?" Delia said.

"I'm starving, and I love their cook, but I'm also eager to get home. Pass the jerky, and let's keep riding. I bet Fanny will have leftovers aplenty in the kitchen," Tempest said.

"Y'all got a problem with that?" Delia asked Tyrell.

"Not at all," Tyrell said. "Reckon we could sleep in your barn tonight and ride out early tomorrow morning."

"I reckon you'll sleep in a bedroom tonight and stay over another night so we can thank you properly for your protection. Aunt Rachel wouldn't abide any less, and Uncle Jonathan will have to hear a complete report of the past three weeks. It took the stagecoach four weeks to take us out to Texas. You've done well getting us home in less," Delia said, and she kneed her horse forward.

"I'm not agreeing to stay," Micah muttered.

"We can't be rude," Tyrell told him, his heart oddly lighter.

They rode on and reached the plantation house at nine o'clock that night. There was still a light sending forth a glow out of the window in the library when they dismounted. Tempest rushed to the front door first and returned in a few minutes with her arm looped through a tall, dark-haired man's.

Delia and Fairlee both hugged him tightly. They were home at last. They had survived, and embracing their uncle proved it. They weren't dreaming, and life was back to normal.

"Come inside. Leave those horses. Fanny is still in the kitchen. I'll have her send for Samson to take care of the animals. Have you had food? Tempie said you kept riding past the turnoff to Bennett's Bluff. Fanny will set a table for you. I'm Jonathan Lavalle," he said to the men. "Thank you for bringing my nieces home to safety."

"Tyrell Fannin, sir." Tyrell stuck out his hand.

Jonathan Lavalle shook it firmly.

"I'm Tyrell's cousin, Isaac Burnet, sir."

Jonathan shook his hand and turned to Micah.

"And I'm Micah Burnet, Isaac's brother," he said.

Jonathan extended his hand toward Micah, who shook it.

If the house was intimidating with its big white pillars on the outside, it was even more so inside the front door. Jonathan lit a few candles and lamps, and the glow illuminated the fancy legs of the foyer table and the banister of a winding staircase. Expensive carpets covered hardwood floors, and a bowl of fresh fruit sat on the foyer piece.

A lady wearing a white silk wrapper peered

251

down from the top of the stairs. "Jonathan, who's here? I thought I heard voices. Oh, my goodness, is that you, Delia? My, oh, my, we weren't expecting you." She hurried down the steps and hugged all the Lavalle sisters at once.

Delia finally stepped out of the group embrace and said, "Aunt Rachel, these are the men Father hired to escort us home. The Alamo was about to be attacked, and he feared for our safety."

"I'm Tyrell Fannin, ma'am. We were on our way home to our place in Mississippi, and it was on the way. These are my cousins, Isaac and Micah Burnet." He introduced them to Rachel.

"Welcome to Oak View. We're glad to have you. Your rooms will be ready by the time you finish having a late supper. Jonathan, have you told Fanny to take care of things?"

"It's already done."

"Good. Now we'll go to the dining room and visit while you eat." Rachel led the way. The ladies followed her. Jonathan motioned for Tyrell, Isaac, and Micah to go after them, and he brought up the rear.

By the time they were seated, two servants were already setting bowls of soup at six place settings on a table built to seat twenty people. Jonathan sat down at the head of the table, asked for a cup of coffee, and sipped it while the newcomers had their late supper.

Rachel, sitting beside Delia, gave her time to take a few sips before asking questions. "Tell me about the danger at the Alamo."

Delia told the story of Santa Anna's men surrounding San Antonio and her father sending them back to Louisiana.

"We saw Santa Anna," Tempest exclaimed.

Rachel put a hand over her heart. "You mean the battle had already started before you were sent to safety?"

"No, no." Fairlee told the story of how Captain Robert Lavalle went to the jail and enlisted the help of three outlaws to spirit the three sisters out of Texas. When she finished telling how they'd reacted to having to wear nuns' habits for a week and the fit Delia threw, Jonathan was shaking with laughter.

Tyrell wasn't far behind him. He'd never thought about how the Lavalle women would react to having to be nuns. Especially Delia. The way Fairlee told the story of Delia's fit when the captain told her to put on the nun's habit had Tyrell wishing he could have been there.

The servants cleared the soup bowls and replaced them with plates of cold ham, sweet potatoes with a sugar and cinnamon coating, slices of bread, and buttered peas.

"So there we were." Delia picked up where Fairlee left off and told them about encountering Santa Anna and his men and how she was almighty glad they had had habits covering up their trousers and shirts at the time.

"You blessed that man?" Rachel asked.

"Well, not really, but I couldn't curse him either. I am anxious to have news of the Alamo. I don't suppose it's made the newspapers yet, has it?" Delia asked.

"I haven't seen anything. We did have a traveler stop last week who said he was on the way to join up with Sam Houston to do some fighting. That's all," Jonathan said.

"Tell us more. You've only told us about the first few days," Rachel prompted.

Jonathan patted her hand. "Darlin', it's getting late, and these young folks have traveled a long way. Perhaps we should save some details for tomorrow."

"I can't sleep until I've heard at least the bare bones. The details can come along later," Rachel said.

By then the plates had been quietly removed and replaced with saucers holding coconut pie.

"Well, there were the Indians," Tempest

said. "You would have been proud of Delia. She stood right up to the chief. He might have killed her if Tyrell hadn't thought fast and told him that we were all married and traveling together."

Rachel smiled. Her blue eyes glittered, and her round face lit up. "I sure can't sleep without knowing how you got out of that one. It gives me the vapors just thinking of you girls traveling through such wild country."

Tempest went on to tell the story and had Rachel clucking her tongue at the treatment of poor little Hannah and wiping her eyes at the end when they found her parents.

"And there was a tornado," Micah piped up, enjoying himself far more than he had thought possible when he saw the outside of the Lavalle family home.

Tyrell shot him a look that said it was the ladies' homecoming and they should relate the incidents the way they wanted. But Micah chose to ignore it when Jonathan asked him to tell the story.

When he finished, Tempest took center stage again. "And then there was the baby I found." She described the sad scene and the miracle of the childless Cunninghams.

Rachel shook her head slowly. "Don't a one of you ever mention that part to Rosy.

She'll fuss the rest of her life if you do. I might do some fussin' myself over it. A new baby in this old house sure would have livened it up."

Delia shut her eyes and got control of the slow burn fixing to put high color into her cheeks. While Tempest had told the story of the baby, she herself had entertained notions of what a child with her blue eyes and Tyrell's angular features would look like.

"Aunt Rachel, do you know what these men told us when they found out we weren't nuns anymore?" Delia asked, mainly to distract herself from her own musings.

Tyrell didn't know whether to smile or run.

Isaac had been enjoying the fun; too bad it was about to end.

Micah had been looking forward to a bed and more good food. He groaned at the thought of sleeping with his saddle for a pillow.

Rachel shook her head.

"Well, you know that part about Jesus turning water into wine? They said this was the reverse situation. That we had been 'wine' when we were nuns, and then we were 'water,' which was plain old women."

Rachel laughed. "Sounds like they're all three pretty smart. Not a one of you three is ever going to be 'wine,' not with your mother and father's blood flowing through your veins. Those two were born to adventure. Now, that's probably enough for one night. Don't forget the rest of the trip, and tell it to me over breakfast. Poor Mr. Fannin's eyes are drooping. We'll all retire now if you've had enough food to hold you until breakfast."

"Yes, ma'am, we surely have been fed well for a bunch of 'outlaws,' " Tyrell said.

"Oh, posh, you were never real outlaws. You were just rowdy boys full of temper. You had to work it out somewhere. I raised boys — I know how their minds work. Now get on to bed, and tomorrow Jonathan will take you around the place and show you how it runs. The girls and I will get ready for a social tomorrow night to celebrate their being home safely. Nothing fancy — just a few friends," Rachel assured them.

"We thought we'd probably go on home tomorrow morning," Isaac said. *God Almighty in heaven above.* He did not want to stay at Oak View for a "social." He was more than a little backward-feeling at one in his own neck of the woods among people he knew. Just thinking about being subjected to a bunch of fancy strangers was enough to make him stutter.

Rachel threw up her hands. "Nonsense! One more day won't make a lick of difference. We'd be honored if you'd stay a week and let us show you a real party."

Tyrell nodded politely. "One more day, but then we really must go. We're as eager to get to our place as these young women were to arrive here. But we'd love to stay tomorrow and see the plantation, Mr. Lavalle."

"Call me Jonathan. Are you an early riser?"

"Yes, I am," Tyrell said.

"Good, we'll breakfast at daybreak, and I'll have our horses ready to ride right after that. Good night, now. I'll take care of a few more things in the library and then be up, Rachel. You'll show these young men to their rooms?"

Rachel nodded. "They can have the north wing. There are three suites in that area." That would be the proper place to put the menfolk, since the girls had always occupied the south wing of the house. They might have had to live in primitive conditions on the trail, but they were home now, and proper etiquette would be upheld.

"You girls go on and get your baths. I'll be in to tell you good night in a moment," Rachel said at the top of the steps, and she led the men in the opposite direction. "While you men ate, I had baths taken to your rooms. There's robes you can use that were left by my sons. Please make yourselves at home. We are so grateful to you for bringing our girls home safely."

"Thank you," Tyrell said formally.

"I do wish you would reconsider and stay a week or more. Now, have a good night. Jonathan will have great fun showing you the plantation tomorrow." She left them standing before three opened doors.

"Got a preference?" Tyrell asked.

The others shook their heads.

"Then I'll take the one on this side of the hall."

He walked into a huge room with a small fire burning in the fireplace, just enough to take off the evening chill. The clothing from his saddlebags had already been hung in the wardrobe with the door slightly ajar so he could see where they were. An oval tub was filled with water and sitting in front of the fireplace. The bed was a tall four-poster with what looked like a mattress made of the stuff God made clouds from.

He'd barely removed his shirt when a gentle knock made him look at the door. A servant appeared before he could cross the room and asked if he would need help with his bath or getting ready for bed.

"I can take care of it, thank you," Tyrell said.

"Yes, sir," the man said.

Tyrell noticed the tray on the desk when he was drying his body. On it sat a nice, thick chunk of yellow cheese and a piece of coconut pie, along with a china pot filled with coffee.

For Delia and her sisters to have come from such splendor and then performed the way they did on the trail was absolutely amazing.

Rachel buzzed into Delia's room and sat down on a chair while Delia stripped out of her dirty things and stepped into the tub. "You are too thin, darlin'. You've lost weight since you left. I'm afraid none of your dresses will fit you properly. Thank goodness we've given up that tight-waisted style, or it would show for sure. What did you think of those young men? Which one would you choose as your favorite?"

"Aunt Rachel! They're outlaws."

"Posh. You were 'angels.' Neither one of you was labeled rightly, now, were you?

"Well, I can see that you aren't going to answer me tonight, so I'll go on and check on your sisters. I'm so glad you're all home safely. I've worried so about you off in that wild country. Texas is no place for refined women. Good night, my dear."

"Good night, Aunt Rachel," Delia said. Why in heck was everyone in such a hurry for her to be paired off with someone? She groaned, thinking of the upcoming spring social season. She'd be slung right back into the very thing she'd been hoping to escape when she convinced her sisters that their father needed them.

While she worried that their father might need them now more than ever, she also hoped that Samuel Leblanc and Andrew Trudeaux had both already found wives and that Matthew Cheval had dropped off the face of the earth to be devoured by mountain lions or rats. But then, no self-respecting rat would eat Matthew. That would be cannibalism.

She wrinkled her nose as she thought of him and his slimy ways. He wasn't anything at all like Tyrell Fannin. Matthew couldn't be trusted an inch. Tyrell could be trusted through eternity.

CHAPTER SEVENTEEN

Tyrell and the Burnets were not completely socially inept. They'd lived on a large farm or small plantation — whatever the difference was — their whole lives. When their mothers were alive, there were Sunday afternoon socials, spring parties, and fall festivals. So the evening social after supper wasn't anything new except for the fancier guests.

Their clothing had been laundered and ironed and their boots polished. They were dressed and sitting in the library with Jonathan discussing the pros and cons of farming tobacco along with cotton.

"I hear the guests arriving, so we'd best go on out and be nice. Rachel loves company. I must say I'm more of a hermit, but she makes me come out of hiding every chance she gets." Jonathan smiled.

The front door of the house opened into the large foyer with the winding staircase.

On the left a doorway opened into a formal living room, with the dining room and kitchen beyond that. To the right of the stairs was a hallway leading to the library, lined on two sides with bookcases, windows looking out over the front lawn on another, and a doorway into a private study on the fourth wall.

When Tyrell reached the foyer, Rachel introduced him and his cousins to the first of their guests, the Chevals from the next plantation. Matthew was younger than Tyrell and sized him up like a tomcat looking at a rival. His mother and father were close to the same age as Rachel and Jonathan but appeared to be a standoffish couple who didn't smile very often. Mrs. Cheval was as round as she was tall and wore a green dress trimmed in black. Mr. Cheval was built the same way as his wife. Tyrell wondered how they had gotten a tall, sissified-looking son from a mix of the two of them.

"Well, well," Matthew Cheval said loudly enough that Tyrell turned and followed his gaze upward.

Delia held the staircase rail with one hand and clasped a thin shawl around her shoulders with the other. Delia in a dress was even more than his dreams had promised. The garment was the same color blue as the summer sky and her eyes, trimmed in a darker velvet ribbon tied under her bosom. Her arms were bare except for the faintest of puffed sleeves and the shawl, which only teased at covering her skin.

Tyrell was glad he didn't have to speak, because his mouth was as dry as desert sand. When Delia was halfway down the steps, Fairlee appeared behind her. She wore a dark blue dress styled the same way as Delia's and trimmed in white ribbons. Her hair was styled in ringlets around her face and a discreet roll at her neck. Delia had made it to the bottom of the stairs when Tempest started down. Her dress was scarlet trimmed in pale pink, and her shawl was a floral creation of the two colors.

But Tyrell didn't really see anyone but Delia. She flashed him a lovely smile when she caught his eye, and the feeling in his heart was bittersweet. He'd found love and couldn't have her. Part of his heart would always be hers. He'd have to be careful not to visit that part too often or stay too long, or he'd never find a wife.

"Good afternoon, Mr. and Mrs. Cheval, Matthew. Have you met Tyrell Fannin and his cousins?" Delia asked.

Tyrell was especially handsome that evening in his crisply ironed shirt and shiny boots. He'd shaved, and his eyes sparkled. She'd love to tuck her arm into his and let him lead her into the parlor. Suddenly she wished that she was wearing trousers and riding a horse so that she didn't have to be a lady.

Matthew rushed to her side so fast that he almost stumbled. "Yes, of course we have, and we are so grateful that these good men have brought you home to us. I've been so worried about you, my dear." He took her hand and brought it to his lips.

Tyrell fought the urge to flatten his nose.

Delia swiftly removed her hand and turned back to Tyrell. "Shall we go into the parlor? Aunt Rachel has refreshments laid out, and you all can get to know these outlaws who escorted us home from Texas."

"You can tell them about your adventures," Rachel said.

Fairlee gave Matthew a brilliant smile and looped her arm through his. "Of course we will. Come along, Matthew. We've had a horrendous three weeks. When everyone else arrives, we'll tell you all about it."

"Who else will be here, Aunt Rachel?" Tempest asked.

"The Cassadies are invited and the Holmans. They both sent a message that . . . Oh, I hear a carriage. They must be arriving now. They were coming along together. The Holmans have been visiting the Cassadies this week. That will make a nice little gathering." Rachel and Jonathan headed toward the door while the sisters led the Chevals into the parlor.

Tyrell was glad that the Cassadies and Holmans didn't bring along a son or a nephew or even an acquaintance like Matthew. The man looked like a vulture waiting for his prey to die so he could pluck its eyes out. But was Delia that prey? He shuddered inwardly.

At Rachel's prompting, the story of their escapades was retold, taking up most of the evening and entertaining the guests quite well. They all shared their concerns about Captain Robert Lavalle. Ruby and Terrance Cassady were the neighbors to the south, their place lying close to the Red Chute Bayou — about an hour and a half by carriage, from what Tyrell learned. The Holmans lived in New Orleans and had known the Lavalle sisters' mother before she married Captain Lavalle. Daisy Holman was Ruby's cousin. She and her husband, Luke, came to visit once a year in the spring. Keeping names and intertwining relationships straight was difficult when all Tyrell really wanted to do was take Delia outside and tell her how he felt.

Matthew Cheval listened to the stories the sisters told, but he hung on Delia's words, as if they were manna from heaven. Tyrell quickly determined that something wasn't totally right. The man appeared to be engrossed in what Delia was saying. He smiled at the right times, laughed when the tale was funny, wiped his forehead when Tempest told about falling into the trap. But his brown eyes seemed to have a heavy curtain over them, and no life showed through.

At the end of two hours, Rachel directed everyone to the refreshment table, where cheeses, dried fruit, and cold cuts were laid out. She invited the whole crowd to stay for the night, but excuses were made. The men retreated to the library for drinks, and the women went back to the parlor.

Mrs. Cheval patted Delia on the hand and whispered, "Matthew has missed you, dear."

"I missed everyone," Delia said. "But I fear for my father. We've made light of the trip and all our harrowing experiences, but I'm afraid the Alamo had no chance against so many Mexican solders. I will be so glad when we have word that Father is safe."

"I'm sure you will," Rachel said. Then she changed the subject. Thinking about losing

Robert so soon after Rosetta was obviously more than she wanted to think about. "When are you all having your spring parties this year? We really must coordinate our times so that they're not in the same week."

"Maybe I shall stay through Ruby's, if it's not too far in the future," Daisy said.

"Then you should plan the first one, Ruby," Rachel said.

"I'm thinking about two weeks from now. The first of April. Perhaps a masquerade. Those are always fun," Ruby said.

The talk stayed on the topic of their spring parties, while Delia's mind wandered in another direction. Tomorrow would be the last time she'd see Tyrell. He'd looked so handsome that evening in his freshly washed and ironed clothing. His hair was too long, of course, but all evening she'd caught herself wanting to reach out and touch those curls, tangle her hands in them to see if they were as soft as they looked.

In the library Jonathan offered the men cigars and brandy. Matthew Cheval was the first one in line for both. Tyrell stepped to the windows and looked out over manicured lawns, azaleas in bloom, and trimmed shrubs.

Matthew had lit up a cigar when he joined

Tyrell at the window. "Don't you want a cigar or a brandy?"

"Not tonight," Tyrell answered.

"Why not?"

"I need a good night's sleep, and brandy gives me dreams," he said.

"You're missing a good drink. Jonathan only keeps the best. What are you looking at?" Matthew squinted to see if perhaps Delia had gone for an evening stroll out on the lawn.

"Just the moonlight on the flowers," Tyrell said.

"Nice, isn't it?"

"Very," Tyrell said.

"What really happened on that trip?"

"I think the ladies shared most of the details," Tyrell said.

"You mean to tell me that the three of you men didn't take advantage of the situation?" Matthew asked.

"For that slur, I could call you out," Tyrell said. "We were paid to do a job. We did it. That's all there is."

"Good, because I'm going to marry Delia Lavalle. I'm asking her at the first spring party this year. I'm hoping to have a summer wedding," he said.

"You're confident that she'll say yes?" Tyrell asked.

"Of course. She's past twenty. Her options are slimming on a daily basis," Matthew said softly.

"Does her uncle approve?"

"Delia is of age. She doesn't need the old man's approval," Matthew hissed.

"Do you love her?"

"What's that got to do with anything? I'll be a good husband. I'll make sure she has what she needs."

"And what if she says no?" Tyrell asked.

"She won't. Her reputation is tainted whether she wants to admit it or not. She's rebelled long enough. It's time someone tamed her, and I'm just the man to do it," Matthew said.

"I see," Tyrell said.

"My father is motioning that it's time for us to say goodbye. Thank you for bringing her home safely, even with a few marks of doubt surrounding her. That her reputation isn't as shiny as a silver platter might work on my behalf. If you lived closer, I'd invite you to the wedding. Tell me, you must have at least lusted in your mind after one of the girls. Which one was it?"

"As I said, it was a job. Good night, Mr. Cheval," Tyrell said firmly.

The Holmans and the Cassidies left at the same time the Cheval family did. Tyrell,

Isaac, and Micah said their good nights, offered thanks to the Lavalles for their hospitality, told them they'd be leaving before first light, and said a round of good-byes.

Delia dressed for bed but couldn't sleep. She paced the floor and looked out the windows. She heard the clock chime three times in the library. Within two hours Tyrell would be leaving forever. The thought of it brought tears to her eyes and a lump to her throat.

"It's only because we were together twenty-four hours a day every single day. I can get over this," she murmured as she paced from one end of her bedroom to the other.

She sat down on the settee close to the window and propped her arms on the sill. It was there that she fell asleep, and she awoke when she heard horses' hooves riding away from Oak View. She jerked her head up and watched the men leave with tears in her eyes.

Tyrell was gone.

She dressed for the day in a simple yellow cotton dress, wrapped a white shawl around her shoulders, and went to the kitchen. Fanny and Rosy were busy making breakfast.

Rosy looked up at Delia with a question in her ebony eyes. Miss Delia was the earliest riser of any of the girls, often up even before Mr. Jonathan, but it was much too early for any of them to be up and about after company the night before.

"What brings you to the kitchen at this hour?" Rosy asked.

"Did they have breakfast before they left?"

"Those good-lookin' menfolk? No, ma'am. Fanny wrapped up some ham and cheese and bread and sent it along with them. They's in a powerful hurry to be on their way. They's women must be waitin' on them," Rosy said.

"Need some help?" Delia asked the women.

"Mr. Jonathan is partial to your pancakes. You could make 'em this mornin'," Rosy suggested.

"You're just giving me something to keep me busy," Delia said.

"Devil gets after folks who don't keep busy."

"Rosy, did he say anything before he left?"

"Which one? They's three of 'em."

"The oldest one. The one who is the cousin to the brothers."

"Oh, that Tyrell Fannin. Now he's a fine-lookin' man. If'n I was a white woman, I wouldn'ta let him go ridin' off like that, but I ain't. I'm an old woman, and what does an old woman know anyway?" she fussed as Fanny fried ham and whipped up eggs.

"Did he say anything at all?" Delia pressed.

"Yes'm. He said thank you for ever'thing. You let him ride outta here, Miss Delia, and now you got a heavy heart. Sometimes you got to reach out and do some takin' 'stead of waitin' for it to be handed to you," Rosy told her.

"Guess there's a time for taking and a time for letting go. Today is my time for letting go. Sometimes it's not so easy, is it?"

"Never is easy. I'd say you got about an hour 'fore he's so far gone you'd never catch him 'fore he got home," Rosy said.

Delia shook her head slowly. "I can wear trousers and skin a rabbit. I can't make a man love me."

"Don't reckon you can. But you can tell him you love *him,*" Rosy said.

Delia sighed. "I'm not that brazen."

Tyrell and his cousins stopped at noon. They'd ridden hard, and he figured they'd already put at least twelve or thirteen miles behind them. If they could keep up that speed, it wouldn't take a week for them to

273

make it to Greenville.

They made a quick noon camp beside a small stream flanked with willow trees hanging with gray, feathery moss. There was plenty of food left from breakfast for lunch, and Isaac and Micah ate heartily. Tyrell ate because his body needed sustenance to keep going. Nothing tasted good in spite of his hunger.

"Why don't you turn around and go back and get her?" Isaac said.

"She's too good for me," Tyrell told him honestly.

"That's a big lie," Micah said.

"You saw that place. She's been raised rich. We aren't poor, but we don't have that kind of life. I can't give her what she's used to having," Tyrell said.

"You just going to carry that heavy load with you the rest of your life like you did Lucy Adams all those years?" Isaac asked.

"I got over Lucy. I'll get over Delia," Tyrell said stoically.

"Might take years, and by then you'll be so old, you won't ever find a wife," Micah cautioned.

"Maybe so, but I can't offer Delia less than she deserves," Tyrell said. "The horses have eaten and had water. Let's get back into the saddle and ride until dark."

■ ■ ■ ■

Delia went through the day in a state of numbness. She helped Fanny make fresh plum jam in the kitchen and spent an hour in the garden with Rachel deciding where to transplant the roses and whether or not they should put a statue in the middle instead of the gazing ball.

At noon she ate and wondered how far Tyrell and his cousins had made it that morning. Did they stop for noon at an inn? Would he go into a saloon later that day and take a bar-room woman up on her offer, since he was no longer bound to a job?

In the middle of the afternoon, restlessness finally sent her to the stables. She saddled her horse and rode out across the land, stopping several times and looking to the east. No dust devils kicked up. Tyrell wasn't coming back.

That night she claimed she had a headache and asked that a tray be brought to her room. She expected one of the servants to bring it up and was surprised when Tempest and Fairlee opened her bedroom door with it.

"Why did you let him go?" Fairlee asked bluntly.

"Because it's against the law to kidnap a grown man," Delia joked weakly.

"Did you really fall in love?" Tempest asked.

"I'm afraid I did. Now I'll simply have to fall *out* of love."

"Well, Matthew is in love with you," Tempest said.

Delia rolled her blue eyes. "I'd rather live with a rattlesnake."

"Oh, he's not so bad," Fairlee said. "At least he's not ugly."

"He's not as pretty as those Burnets or Tyrell, is he, though?" Tempest said.

"No, but Matthew's close to home, and he's already got a nice plantation." Fairlee took up for him.

"Which is falling down around his ears and which he needs a rich wife to keep afloat," Tempest rattled on.

"How do you know all that?" Fairlee asked.

"Remember, my major failing — well, other than temper — is that I eavesdrop," Tempest said.

Delia was just glad for the conversation to be off Tyrell. If she heard his name again or imagined that she saw him standing there again or thought about those kisses they'd shared one more time, she was sure to break down and sob.

Fairlee laughed aloud. "Delia's failing is that she can't tell a lie to save her neck. I was sure we'd throw those habits into the river long before a week was up, but she'd promised Father, and she couldn't let that be a lie. You have fits and eavesdrop. If we want to know something, we can always find out through you. Who'd you hear saying those things about Matthew Cheval?"

Tempest ignored her and pointed at Delia. "Eat, or I'm tellin' Rosy, and she'll send up that vile medicine to cure you." She turned toward Fairlee. "And *your* failing is that you can't keep a secret, so I'm not telling you who said it, but trust me, it's the truth as solid as the gospel. Matthew Cheval needs a rich wife. He doesn't want one, but if he doesn't marry one soon, his debtors are going to take him to prison."

Delia ate enough supper to keep Tempest from tattling to Rosy and then sent her sisters to their rooms. She was about to shed her dress and retire when she heard the thunder of horse hooves, so she peered out the window.

When she saw that it wasn't her imagination and was indeed a horse, she ran out of the room and down the stairs in her bare feet. She threw open the front door and was on the porch when the horse came to a stop and the rider hopped off and immediately fell to one knee in front of her.

"Will you marry me, Delia Lavalle?" he said.

She took a deep breath to calm her racing heart and looked down at the man, all the while thinking how stupid he looked. "No, I will not!" she said.

"But why?"

"I do not love you, Matthew Cheval. Why are you back here already?"

"Because I've thought about it all day, and I couldn't wait another moment. I was afraid that you'd run off with that farmer. I should have taken you aside last night or at least asked your uncle for permission to court you. Please say you'll marry me." Matthew continued to beg as he stood. He grabbed her hand, bringing it to his lips.

"I won't marry without love," Delia said.

"You can learn to love me," he said.

"What if I didn't? What if I made you miserable?" she asked.

"I'm willing to take that chance."

"I'm not. I won't marry without love, and I do not love you, so the answer is still no. I'm going back inside now."

He grabbed her arm. "You'll be sorry. You

are a tainted woman. All those weeks on that trip with those three men. People will talk about you, whisper behind your back. Even if nothing happened between you, there will always be that doubt. No one will want you, Delia. You're ruined. I'm willing to give you a name and restore your reputation."

She jerked her arm free and started into the house. "Then I'll be the old maid with a past. I appreciate your generous offer, Matthew, but I will not marry you. Now please leave."

"Someday you'll wish you'd married me. I'll see to it that you'll regret your decision," Matthew said.

"Don't threaten me," she said coldly.

He jumped onto his horse and rode away as if the devil were kissing the horse's tail. "That's not a threat. It's a promise," he shouted.

"Guess you took care of that," a voice said from the deep shadows on the other end of the porch.

Delia could have sworn it was Tyrell's voice, but then, she'd thought she'd seen him several times that day, only to realize when she blinked that it was a trick of the light.

"So you don't love him, and you won't

marry without it?" he asked.

She took two steps into the darkness, and, sure enough, there Tyrell sat, on the far edge of the porch.

"Where did you come from?"

"Oh, I've been here a while, trying to get up the courage to toss a pebble at your window," he said.

"I didn't hear your horse."

"Didn't want you to."

"Why'd you come back?"

"For you."

Her heart stopped and then picked up a head of steam and raced ahead so fast that she thought it would hop out of her chest.

"Why?" she whispered, still not so sure that she wasn't dreaming.

"Fell in love with you back there on the road. Can't imagine living without you. But all I've got is a farm about half this big and my heart to offer you." Tyrell spoke softly.

"I'd be satisfied with your love and your heart," she said.

"Then I reckon I'm asking you if you'd marry me and come to Mississippi with me," he said.

She didn't hesitate. She walked right into his open arms and pressed her cheek against his chest. "Yes. I fell in love with you along that trail too."

His arms folded around her.

Using the knuckles of one hand, he tilted her chin up and kissed her. "Reckon we could wed tomorrow. I've got a farm to run. We could take the stagecoach that comes through here and honeymoon along the way. It's the best I can offer at the moment."

"For another one of those kisses, I'll elope with you tonight," she said.

"Wouldn't ask you to do that. We'll do it right tomorrow, but here's another one anyway." He kissed her again.

CHAPTER EIGHTEEN

"If you'd wait a month, we could have a proper wedding. It would be the end of April, and the magnolias would be in bloom. We could have a proper dress designed." Rachel fussed as she pinned dogwood blossoms into Delia's hair.

"Won't you please stay here for a while? Let Tyrell go on, and you can follow with your things when they're packed and ready to be shipped," Tempest begged. She'd been more than ready for Delia to marry, but not for her sister to move more than a hundred miles away.

Delia adjusted the neckline of her pale pink dress. "I'm getting married today, and I'm leaving after we have some of Fanny's lovely cake. Tyrell and I will honeymoon across the state of Louisiana. We're going in the stagecoach, just like I told you all this morning at breakfast. Please send my horse along with my things when you get the wagon packed with them. I can't believe Uncle Jonathan is sending Rosy too. I'm so excited that she's coming to live with us."

"Rosy wants to go. She says these two won't ever find men willin' to take on their sass, and she wants to help raise one more generation of Lavalles before she dies," Rachel said.

Fairlee giggled. "Y'all better hurry up. Rosy is gettin' old."

Delia smiled. "I'm thinking maybe I'll have a houseful of boys to torment their old-maid aunts when they come around to visit."

"Old maid? I'm getting married by Christmas!" Fairlee declared.

"I'll believe it when I see it," Delia said.

"But we've never been apart," Tempest whined.

"You can come with me. You said you wanted to visit our cousins. Well, visit me instead."

"I will, but it won't be the same," Tempest whimpered.

"You'll have to come and see us here. I vowed I wasn't leaving home again, and I'm not," Fairlee said.

"Okay, it's a deal. Once a year I'll come for a week during party season. How's that? And I'll bring my sons to torment you here."

"If that's the best you can offer, it'll have to do," Fairlee said.

The clock chimed four times.

"Let's go," Delia said with a brilliant smile. "Be happy for me. I love Tyrell. It took nearly losing him to make me admit it."

Tempest shuddered. "And a proposal from that horrid Matthew Cheval."

"I keep telling you both, he's not so bad," Fairlee argued as they made their way single file down the stairs.

Delia stopped and looked at her sister. "He's terrible. Promise me you won't ever marry anyone like that."

"I will never marry a terrible person." Fairlee twisted the words a bit, and from the look of relief on Delia's face, she'd done a fine job of it.

Tyrell and Delia stood before the preacher in the parlor and repeated their vows. He slipped the gold band onto her finger that her mother had worn for more than twenty years, and he vowed that he would cherish her until death parted them. The preacher had a few things to say about the symbolism of the eternal band and how that particular ring was special, since it had belonged to Delia's mother, who would be honored to know that her ring was helping begin a new marriage.

Then he pronounced them man and wife.

Tyrell tilted Delia's face up toward his, thrilled to see the love and trust in her eyes.

Later that night the stagecoach stopped at an inn in a small town on the road across northern Louisiana. Tyrell signed the register with *Mr. and Mrs. Tyrell Fannin,* and when they reached their room, he picked her up to carry her over the threshold.

"Please put me down for just a minute. I need to tell you something important before we go through that door."

He set her down and raised an eyebrow.

"I was afraid to tell you before the wedding. I was afraid you'd ride off and leave me again," she said.

"You were married before?" he asked. That was the worst thing he could think of at the moment.

"No. Momma came from very wealthy people. They had — have — this big shipping company. I guess it's *have,* because some of my cousins still run it down in New Orleans." She hesitated. Uncle Jonathan had told her to be honest and tell Tyrell before the wedding, and she'd let her uncle believe that she had. But Tyrell was a proud man, and he'd never want it said that he'd married a woman for her money.

"We — we can always just keep it quiet when we get to Mississippi," she stammered.

Tyrell put his arms around her and said, "Why don't you just spit out whatever you want to say, darlin'?"

"When Momma came to Oak View, she brought this enormous dowry with her. But Daddy was a proud man and wouldn't touch the money, so it was put into a trust fund for us three girls. Upon marriage or when we turn twenty-five, it's ours. It's quite a bit, and I'm afraid you'll be too proud to share it with me. But what good is it if we don't use it to build whatever we want together? Please don't be angry with me, but I was afraid you'd leave and never come back because you wouldn't want me to think you were marrying me for the money." She talked so fast and furiously that she had to inhale deeply to refill her lungs.

Tyrell laughed. "I love you, Delia Fannin. I don't care if all you have are the clothes on your back or if you have enough money to buy the whole state of Louisiana. Leaving you isn't an option. I'd be leaving my heart, and I can't live without it or you. I was scared to death I'd waited too late when

Cheval rode up and proposed all proper like on one knee. And then I was terrified because I didn't have a ring. But your Uncle Jonathan said you should be married with your mother's ring. Guess we both had our share of fears today."

She snuggled against his broad chest. "But it's over now, isn't it?"

"It is. I love you, Delia."

"Even though I'm not a real angel?"

"Honey, I knew the first time I looked into your eyes that you couldn't be a nun. I just couldn't explain why that first week."

She pulled his mouth down to hers for a kiss. "How?"

"Because I smelled smoke," he whispered into her ear.

The warmth of his breath made her shiver. "Smoke?"

"Sure. From the beginning you had one wing in the fire," he teased.

"From wine to water," she said.

"And man cannot live without water," he whispered as he carried her into the room and kicked the door shut.